"FAITH-BASED FICTION DOESN'T GET
BETTER THAN BILLINGSLEY'S"
raves *Publishers Weekly*. . . . And *Library Journal*
says her storytelling "will appeal to fans of Michele
Andrea Bowen's *Second Sunday* and Pat G'Orge-
Walker's *Sister Betty! God's Calling You, Again!*"

**Acclaim for the novels of #1 bestselling author
ReShonda Tate Billingsley!**

A GOOD MAN IS HARD TO FIND

"Billingsley's engaging voice will keep readers turning the pages and
savoring each scandalous revelation."

—*Publishers Weekly* (starred review)

HOLY ROLLERS

"Sensational. . . . [Billingsley] masterfully weaves together her trade-
mark style of humor, girl-next-door drama, faith, and romance . . .
[and] makes you fall in love with these characters."

—*Romantic Times Book Review*

THE DEVIL IS A LIE

"Steamy, sassy, sexy. . . . An entertaining dramedy [that] will keep
readers laughing—and engrossed." —*Ebony*

"Billingsley delivers a romantic page-turner dipped in heavenly
goodness." —*Romantic Times* (4½ stars)

"Fast moving and hilarious." —*Publishers Weekly*

Don't miss these high-spirited novels featuring
Rachel Adams, and set in the unforgettable
Houston congregation of *Say Amen, Again*!

EVERYBODY SAY AMEN
A *USA Today* Top Ten Summer Sizzler!

"Packed with colorful characters, drama, and scandal. . . . A fun, redemptive book."
                                            —*Romantic Times*

LET THE CHURCH SAY AMEN
#1 *Essence* magazine bestseller
One of *Library Journal*'s Best Christian Books for 2004

"Billingsley infuses her text with just the right dose of humor to balance the novel's serious events."   —*Library Journal* (starred review)

"Amen to *Let the Church Say Amen*. . . . [A] well-written novel."
                                            —*Indianapolis Recorder*

"Emotionally compelling. . . . Full of palpable joy, grief, and soulful characters."   —*The Jacksonville Free Press* (FL)

"Her community of very human saints will win readers over with their humor and verve."   —*Booklist*

ReShonda Tate Billingsley's novels are also
available as eBooks

Also by ReShonda Tate Billingsley

A Good Man Is Hard to Find
Holy Rollers
The Devil Is a Lie
Can I Get a Witness?
The Pastor's Wife
Everybody Say Amen
Have a Little Faith
(with Jacquelin Thomas, J. D. Mason and Sandra Kitt)
I Know I've Been Changed
Help! I've Turned Into My Mother
Let the Church Say Amen
My Brother's Keeper

And check out ReShonda's young adult titles

Drama Queens
Caught Up in the Drama
Friends 'Til the End
Fair-Weather Friends
Getting Even
With Friends Like These
Blessings in Disguise
Nothing But Drama

say amen, again

ReShonda Tate Billingsley

GALLERY BOOKS

New York   London   Toronto   Sydney

GALLERY BOOKS
A Division of Simon & Schuster, Inc.
1230 Avenue of the Americas
New York, NY 10020

First Gallery Books trade paperback edition July 2011

GALLERY BOOKS and colophon are registered trademarks of Simon & Schuster, Inc.

For information about special discounts for bulk purchases, please contact Simon & Schuster Special Sales at 1-866-506-1949 or business@simonandschuster.com.

The Simon & Schuster Speakers Bureau can bring authors to your live event. For more information or to book an event contact the Simon & Schuster Speakers Bureau at 1-866-248-3049 or visit our website at www.simonspeakers.com.

Manufactured in the United States of America

10 9 8 7

Library of Congress Cataloging-in-Publication Data

Billingsley, ReShonda Tate.
    Say amen, again / by ReShonda Tate Billingsley. — 1st Gallery Books trade paperback ed.
        p. cm.
    1. African American clergy—Fiction. 2. African American families—Fiction. I. Title.
    PS3602.I445S29 2011
    813'.6—dc22   2010043778

ISBN 978-1-4165-7806-2
ISBN 978-1-4165-7818-5 (ebook)

"... You know you've found
your passion when you'd do
what you do for free ..."

A Note from the Author

I travel the country, touring and speaking. One of the questions I'm asked the most is, "How did you know writing was something you wanted to do?" Besides the fact that I've been writing for as long as I can remember, I get tremendous joy at just the simple thought of crafting the perfect sentence, letting my words dance on the paper, and allowing my imagination to run rampant. The bottom line is, I would write for free.

The great thing is I don't have to.

I continue to marvel at the fact that somebody is actually paying me to do this!

Don't get me wrong, I work hard—just ask my family. But when you're doing what you love, loving what you do, work just doesn't feel as hard.

But I know that I wouldn't be able to do any of it were it not for God's grace and my incredible support system. Hence, the reason that I have to yet again take a moment to say thanks to those people who make my world go round, who entertain my discussions about fictitious people, who step up to the plate when

A Note from the Author

I'm constantly stepping out on the road, who understand when I have to miss lunches, parties, showers and events because duty calls, and who say "Dang, you want me to buy another book?" right before shelling out some more of their hard-earned cash.

My family, who catches it the most. My supportive husband, Miron, and my three wonderful children. Thank you so much for putting up with the travel, the hectic schedule and the never-ending deadlines. All that I do is for you.

To my mother, Nancy Bea (quit cussing about me using your country name), I know you are CONSTANTLY reminding me that I'm gonna "be in a world of trouble when you leave this earth" but that's a fact that I don't need reminding of (not that you'd stop anyway). One day I'm gonna blow up and make all your efforts worthwhile. To my sister, Ta-Tanisha . . . eternal gratitude to you as well for . . . well, everything. I'm gonna hook you up, too . . . one of these days.

My ride-or-die girls, who I know want to curse me out because of my busy schedule but never stop loving and supporting me nonetheless: Jaimi Canady, Raquelle Lewis, Kim Wright, Clemelia Richardson, Tammy Smithers, Kristi King and Finisha Woodson. And to my other Delta Xi sorors, you know I have mad love for you even if I'm not listing everyone's names.

Pat Tucker Wilson. Words can't describe how lucky I am to call you a friend. Thanks for everything!

Fay Square and LaWonda Young, it's so wonderful to have caring people like you in my life to make my job so much easier.

The literary people who make my career what it is: Sara Camilli, Brigitte Smith, John Paine, Melissa Gramstad,

A Note from the Author

Andrea DeWerd, Louise Burke and the entire staff at Simon & Schuster/Gallery Books!

To my dear friend, Victoria Christopher Murray, it is a joy not only working with you, but traveling on this literary journey with you as well. I can't wait for everyone to read *Saints and Sinners*. To my other colleagues in this literary game, thanks for your constant support: Nina Foxx, Kimberla Lawson Roby, Al Frazier, J. D. Mason, Tiffany Warren, Dee Stewart, Pat G'Orge-Walker, Trice Hickman, Yasmin Coleman, Monica Marie Jones and Rhonda McKnight. And my wonderful assistant, Kym Fisher . . . you are a Godsend!

My Hollywood journey has been an experience to say the least. But it's one I wouldn't trade for anything. I've learned so much about the movie industry as my team works to bring several of my books to the screen. So, thanks once again to Regina King and Reina King for your unwavering dedication and to Bobby Smith, Jr. for your persistence.

Major love to my sorors from the Houston metropolitan chapters, particularly my chapter, Mu Kappa Omega, as well as my sister-moms of the Sugar Land/Missouri city chapter of Jack and Jill.

Thank you to all the wonderful book clubs, bookstores and libraries that have supported my books.

I have to also give thanks to: Yolanda Latoya Gore, Rochelle Scott, Jodi Massey, Carla Rogers, Venetric Lewis, Addie Heyliger, Arnesha Fuqua, Cale Carter, Tee C. Royal, Tasha Martin, Candace K, Tanisha Webb, Radiah Hebert, Curtis Bunn, Isiah Carey and Gwen Richardson.

A Note from the Author

Thanks so much to my wonderful castmates from *Marriage Material,* the play . . . it was a blast working with you: Jill Marie Jones, Michael Colyar, Tank (does this count for putting you in the book?), Patrice Lovely (NOW, can I have the video?), Kier Spates, Tionne "T-Boz" Watkins, Allen Payne, JeCaryous Johnson, Gary Guidry . . . and our protector, Darrell Muhammad.

And I know I should be wrapping up, but I've got to send a shout-out to some special "social" friends. They say Facebook is so impersonal, but I've met some wonderful people who have encouraged, supported and uplifted me on a regular basis. So thank you so much to: Bettie, Jackie, Sheryl, Dasaya, Jerrode, Cami, Jacquelyn, Sylvia, Tonia, Sheretta, Jetola, Mimi, Tati, Alicia, Tres, Phaedra, Lynn, Josie, Raquel, Diane, Portia, Porsha, Shari, Hiawatha, Corey, Tari, Barbara, Catherine, Cherlisa, Alvin, Kim, Patrice, Monique, Maurice, Gigi, Kimmie, Willa, Deborah and Cordia. (I know this seems like a lot . . . but I have thousands of FB friends, so relatively speaking . . .)

Last, but certainly not least, my biggest thanks goes to you, the reader. Thank you for your continued support!

When I sat down to pen the first book in the Amen series, I never intended to write more than one book. But I'm a firm believer in giving the people what they want and enough of you told me that you want to see the Jackson clan again . . . so whether you're a new reader to the series, or continuing to follow their saga, I hope you enjoy . . .

Much Love,

ReShonda

Chapter 1

"Get. It. Out!"

The scream started in Rachel's gut and felt like it traveled up her lungs and out her mouth, piercing the whole room.

"It hurts so bad!" Rachel yelled. Granted, this was her third child, but the pain was like nothing she'd ever experienced. She'd had an epidural on her other two kids. This baby had come too fast for a spinal, and Rachel needed something, because the pain was unbearable.

"Breathe, baby, breathe," Lester—her husband of seven years—said as he leaned over and kissed her forehead.

"Lester, I am breathing," Rachel snapped, pushing him away.

"You can do this," he said soothingly.

"Shut up and get this baby out of me!" she yelled again. He

was the reason she was in this position. She'd had her first child at fifteen. Her second at seventeen. But now, eleven years later, her body wasn't cut out to deliver a baby with the same ease.

Another scream filled the room. Rachel narrowed her eyes in suspicion. That one hadn't come from her. "Lester," she said, reaching for her husband's hand. But he had vanished. She looked over to the other bed in the hospital room.

"Breathe, baby, breathe," Lester said sweetly.

Rachel peered closer. This time Lester wasn't talking to her.

"Come on, Mary, you can do this." He was gently coaxing the woman in the bed next to hers. Unlike Rachel, Mary didn't shoo him away.

"Lester?" Rachel cried. She couldn't believe she was delivering this baby in the bed next to *her,* of all people. Suddenly, Rachel forgot all about the pain shooting through her body. She jumped up and lunged at her husband.

"Hey, let me go! Rachel, what are you doing?"

That was coming from somewhere else, someplace more real. Rachel's eyes shot open. She was in their king-size bed, big belly and all, sitting on top of her husband, her hands gripped firmly around his neck.

Lester scooted back against the headboard, his hands grabbing her wrists. "Why are you trying to choke me?" he panted.

Rachel shook her head, trying to come out of the daze she was in. She looked around. She wasn't in a hospital room. She was in her oversize, Africa-themed bedroom. And she wasn't anywhere near labor.

"Oh, wow," Rachel said, pulling herself up off Lester and

leaning back against the headboard. "I was having a nightmare."

"Again?" Lester said, his voice softening. "Was it the . . ." He stopped, knowing he didn't dare utter the name of the woman that Rachel hated most in the world.

"Yes, it was," Rachel snapped. This was becoming a regular occurrence. It was bad enough that home-wrecking tramp had invaded her marriage. Now Mary Richardson was invading her dreams as well.

"I'm going to make me some hot tea," Rachel said, throwing the covers back.

"Rachel," Lester said, trying to stop her. "Can we talk about this?"

"What is there to talk about?" she said, stepping out of the bed. "It is what it is." She grabbed her robe and wrapped it around her protruding belly. "I'm sure I'm not the only woman in America having nightmares that she's delivering her baby in the same room as her husband's mistress."

Lester groaned. Rachel knew he didn't want to have that argument again, but there was no statute of limitations on her pain. And Lester and that tramp Mary had given her enough pain to last a lifetime.

"Well, at least let me make your tea," he said, climbing out of the bed.

"I got it," she replied, heading toward the door.

"Are you mad at me?" he gently asked.

She gritted her teeth as she stopped in the doorway with her back to him. After seven years of marriage, Lester should have known when to leave well enough alone. She'd needed a whole lot of praying not to revert to her old cut-a-fool ways after Mary had made her stunning announcement—in church, no less—that after a brief affair with Lester, she was pregnant with his child.

That had been the absolute worst, humiliating moment of Rachel's life. Mary, looking like Kim from *The Real Housewives of Atlanta,* standing up in front of the Zion Hill congregation and telling everyone that not only had Pastor Adams been unfaithful but he'd also knocked her up at the same time he'd gotten his wife pregnant. This was the same man who had pursued Rachel relentlessly in high school, who had professed his love for her on a daily basis. She'd finally broken down and given him a chance. She'd cleaned him up, putting him on Proactiv to clear up that horrible acne problem, cutting off that red mop on top of his head, and changing his whole wardrobe from nerdish to stylish. He had shocked her by announcing he'd been called to preach, but then he'd gotten really full of himself and gotten a mistress! The only reason she'd taken him back was that she had some dirt of her own.

Rachel grimaced as she thought back to that horrible day at church. The old Rachel would have snatched Mary's blond wig off, then made her way over to start in on Lester. She'd become a stronger woman, a better First Lady, grown in her walk with God. But Mary seemed determined to make her take a detour with the devil.

It had taken the support of her father, Rev. Simon Jackson, and her brothers, David and Jonathan—who both had drama of their own—to help her get through this ordeal.

At first she'd told Lester to get out, but her father had asked her to pray about it, which she had. And some voice kept telling her to stay with Lester—at least until Mary's baby came and they could have a DNA test. Rachel's pregnancy had been complicated because she had high blood pressure, and Lester had kept wearing her down until she'd finally given in.

"Babe, I can't say it enough. I'm so sorry you're going through this." Lester came up behind her and placed his hands on her waist. She cringed as she felt his fingers. Some days were better than others; she could feel things were as they had been before Mary had come crashing into their worlds. But other days—most days—were like today, when she couldn't stand Lester touching her.

"I know you are," she said without turning around. "Look, I'm going down. I need to be by myself."

"Rach—"

She held up her hand to cut him off. "Not now, Lester."

Rachel walked out of the room before he could say another word. She had to go spend some time by herself, some time in prayer, because as hard as she prayed for God to remove the hate from her heart, He just didn't seem to be working fast enough for her.

Chapter 2

"Girl, I still can't believe you." Bernice Sanders shook her head. She wasn't a churchgoer, but she had come today just to see her friend in action. Mary had sworn it was going to be juicy this morning, and when she sashayed up to the front of the sanctuary—ignoring the glares of almost everyone in the church—Bernice knew she was going to hold true to her word.

"Please. These folks think they got some old scary white girl," Mary whispered as she got comfortable on the second pew. "As Beyoncé says, 'They must not know 'bout me.'"

Mary winked at her friend. She took pleasure in bringing pain to Rev. Lester Adams and his think-she-all-that wife, Rachel. Six months ago, Mary had stood up in the pews to announce she was pregnant with Lester's child. She didn't know what had made her do it. She had just found out the day before and had had every intention of telling Lester that evening. He had already told her that he wanted nothing more to do with her, and Mary had been sure that this news would change his mind. That is, until Lester had stood up with some news of his own. Mary had watched in horror as the good reverend had announced that he and his wife were expecting. Instinctively, she'd risen and made the blockbuster announcement that she was expecting, too. Needless to say, the last six months had been a nightmare with Rachel and all the sanctified folks at Zion Hill acting like she was a pariah. Lester avoided her like the plague. She'd given him his space, but his time was up. It was time for Lester to do right by her and their baby.

During the sermon Mary could tell Bernice was getting restless. She didn't even try to hide her lack of interest during Lester's sermon, because she pulled out her cell phone and began texting someone.

"All right, Bernice, hold on to your hat, because we're about to get this party started," Mary said as Lester went into his benediction.

"So, church, if there is anyone feeling God calling them, please come." Lester stood at the front of the sanctuary, arms outstretched. Zion Hill had seen its share of troubles. Mary hadn't attended under the former pastor—Simon Jackson, Rachel's father. But she'd heard how the church had tried to vote him out because his kids had been so buck wild.

Things had been relatively calm since Lester had taken over when Rev. Jackson's ailing health had forced him into retirement. Well, calm until Mary had shown up. She'd come raging through like a bitter winter storm. And she hadn't vented all her wrath yet.

"Don't stay in your seat. God is calling you. Won't you come now?" Lester continued.

Mary smiled as she stood. She hadn't been back in front of the church since her first visit, when she'd asked the church to pray for her for being involved with a married man. Of course, no one had known that the married man was their beloved pastor, Lester Adams. When she'd announced that she was pregnant, chaos had broken out and she'd been escorted out of the church. She'd given things time to die down, but she was back, and ready to reclaim her man.

Lester's eyes grew wide and nervousness etched his face as Mary made her way to the front of the church. She maintained a tight smile and ignored the grumblings of the members that hated her almost as much as Rachel did. She'd found an ally only in Layla Wilson, the sister-in-law of Rachel's son's father. She couldn't stand Rachel, and that's really all Mary needed.

Mary noticed Rachel out of the corner of her eye. She was shifting uncomfortably as she struggled to contain her disdain. *Wouldn't it be great if I could provoke her enough to come across the aisle and attack me?* Mary thought. She fought to contain her giggle as she imagined the two pregnant women rolling around the altar.

As she expected, Rev. Adams turned the mic over to his assistant pastor, Victor Turner. Pastor Turner eased over to

Mary, who was standing in front of the congregation, her head held high. She knew they hated her, but she didn't care. Lester was the only person that mattered.

"How are you today, Sister Mary?" Pastor Turner said. His voice was stern, like he was sending her a subliminal warning. Pastor Turner had been among the many people who'd tried to get Mary to leave Zion Hill. She'd left, all right, but only until she'd gotten her plan together. And it was more than together now.

Mary smiled knowingly as she took the mic.

"Giving honor to God," Mary said in her most innocent voice, "the leader of my heart." She ignored Rachel's loud coughing. "God has laid it on my heart to ask the church if we could have an unwed mothers ministry. One of the teen members called me last week in tears because she felt like she was being judged." That part was the truth. A fifteen-year-old member named Kayla Brewer had called her at Layla's urging. For Mary, it fit perfectly with her plan. "I sympathized with her feeling isolated. And I definitely know the feeling of being judged all too well," Mary continued.

"You should," someone mumbled from the pews.

"So, I'm hoping that Pastor Adams," Mary smiled at him coyly, "will give his stamp of approval to us starting an unwed mothers ministry. I already have the support of sister Layla Wilson, and I'm sure others will want to get on board. We can make an impact, not only on Zion Hill but on our community at large. We can let these mothers know that hope is not lost just because the fathers of their children are choosing not to be in their lives."

"You have got to be kidding me," Rachel muttered loud enough for everyone to hear.

Mary loved to see Rachel getting worked up, but now wasn't the time to gloat.

"I know the church has a Good Girlz program for troubled teens, and I was thinking maybe we could combine the two," she said, flashing a fake smile. Rachel almost came out of her seat. The Good Girlz was a program Rachel had started, and it was her pride and joy, so Mary knew she'd touched a nerve by even mentioning it.

"A lot of people want to stand in judgment of unwed mothers," Mary continued, "but need I remind everyone that only he who is without sin should cast the first stone. There is no one sin greater than the other."

Pastor Turner quickly took the mic. "All right, Sister Mary. I'm glad that God has placed that on your heart, and I'm sure we can take it before the board and talk about it."

He hurried on to the next person. He'd cut Mary off, but she wasn't upset. Judging from the agitated look on Rachel's face, her work for today was done and her plan was in full swing.

Chapter 3

Lester ducked as the stainless steel frying pan went flying across the room. Two inches to the left and it would have hit him squarely in the forehead. It crashed into the wall, leaving a big gray dent.

"Rachel, would you calm down?" he said, his hands outstretched in a defensive stance. "You know your blood pressure is already high."

"*Calm down?*" she repeated. "After what just happened at church, you want me to be calm?" She picked up another frying pan, their biggest one, and waved it at him. "I was calm during the service when that tramp stood up in front of the church, pretending she really cares about unwed mothers. I was calm when she had the audacity to think I would let her anywhere near my Good Girlz. I was even calm afterward when I had to stand there and fake the funk with everyone offering me their sympathy. But this trick got one more time to try me!" Rachel screamed violently as she waved the frying pan in warning.

Lester took a deep breath as he delivered the speech he'd been giving for the last six months. "We made a vow that we were going to see this through. I know it's difficult for you. But we can—"

"Get her out of the church," Rachel interrupted. Her voice was firm. She had to let Lester know she meant business.

"You know I can't do that. I can't force someone to leave," he protested. "I took it before the board and we have to have a unanimous vote, and . . ."

Rachel knew the "and" was Deacon Jacobs, who'd never cared for Rachel and her family anyway. He kept repeating, "Mary can be redeemed" and even went so far as to say if they kicked one transgressor out, they had to kick them all out.

"Rachel," Lester sighed heavily, "you're the First Lady—"

"Don't go pulling that First Lady card," she snapped, slamming the pan down on the counter. "Right now I'm a woman scorned. No, let me correct that, I'm a pissed-off woman scorned, and if you don't handle her, I will. First Lady or not. Believe that," she said, stomping out of the kitchen. She was no longer in the mood to cook. The kids had gone to a neighbor's birthday party, so Lester would have to fend for himself. He could starve for all she cared.

Rachel grabbed her purse and her keys off the counter as she stormed out of the house and toward her car. She had to leave before she worked herself into a frenzy and went into premature labor.

If only she hadn't been pregnant . . . Rachel blew a deep breath as she backed her Mercedes out of the driveway. No sense in talking about what she would have done if she hadn't been pregnant, because to be honest, she really didn't know. The old Rachel would've left, no questions asked. Yet she'd let Lester explain, and she'd learned it had all been a setup. Mary had purposely seduced Lester. Rachel had been neglecting him because her heart had still been with Bobby, her son's father.

Bobby. The love of her life. The man she felt God had put on this earth just for her. They'd been high school sweethearts, and when she'd ended up pregnant at fifteen, he'd offered to marry her so they could "do right by their son." Bobby had graduated a year before her and they'd planned to get married after Rachel graduated. In the meantime, he'd joined the military to start building a life for them. Only Rachel had been lonely with him being overseas, and Bobby's friend Tony had stepped in to fill that void. One thing had led to another and after one regretful night, Rachel had ended up pregnant again and had soon given birth to a baby girl.

It had been a transgression Bobby had never been able to forgive. Still, Rachel had never stopped trying. She'd been confident that he could learn to love her again. She'd convinced herself that even though he'd married Shante Wilson, a girl who went to their church, his heart was still with her. Ironically, just when Rachel had accepted that she'd never have

Bobby, he'd confessed his love. By that time she'd married Lester, and Bobby's confession had sent her world spiraling out of control. As she'd struggled with her love for Bobby, her doting husband had been left all alone, an easy target.

Rachel recognized the role she had played in the deterioration of her marriage. She had to admit that she'd treated her husband badly, and when she was really honest with herself, she could understand why he would turn to another woman.

Rachel shook off her thoughts. She was not about to go feeling all sympathetic for Lester. Yes, she'd pushed him away, but the fact remained that he'd cheated and could possibly have another child on the way. She had every right to be furious. She had even forgiven Lester for cheating, but that had been before Mary's bombshell announcement. That announcement had changed the game plan. Even if she could forgive, a living, breathing baby would be a constant reminder.

Rachel used her free hand to pull out her cell phone. She punched in the speed dial to call Twyla, her best friend since middle school. "Hey, Twyla, I'm on my way over there," she announced as soon as Twyla picked up.

Even though Twyla hadn't been at church today, Rachel was sure she had heard about Mary by now. Twyla would know exactly what had Rachel so heated up.

"I'll be here," was all Twyla replied.

Fifteen minutes later, Twyla met Rachel at the door with a cup of hot tea.

"I don't want tea." Rachel pushed the cup aside as she brushed past her friend. "I need something stronger."

Say Amen, Again

Twyla used her hip and gently closed the front door. "And after you have your baby, you can have it." She handed Rachel the tea again. "In the meantime, chamomile. It's calming."

Rachel rolled her eyes as she took the cup. She sipped it, not feeling calmed in the slightest, then sat down on the sofa. "Twyla, I swear I'm gonna kill her." She gripped the cup with both hands as she slowly rocked back and forth. "After what that tramp did in church today? Uh-uh, that's justifiable homicide. So, I'm gonna kill her."

"No, you're not," Twyla replied, taking a seat across from her friend.

"Really, I am," Rachel replied. "I was thinking about this on the way over here. Maybe God wants me to lead the prison ministry, you know, from the inside."

"You have two adorable children who need you, and another on the way. So I'm going to assume that's your anger talking." Rachel cut her eyes and Twyla held up her hand. "Don't get me wrong, you have every right to be mad, but murder isn't the answer. Did you pray on it?"

"Yes," Rachel huffed, "and the Lord told me to kill her."

Twyla broke out laughing. "I doubt very seriously that the Lord told you to kill her. That wasn't nobody but the devil."

"Well, the devil is speaking a whole lot louder than God right about now."

"That just means that you need to pray harder," Twyla said.

Rachel rubbed her belly as she rolled her eyes again. She wasn't trying to hear all of that holy talk right now because she was sick of turning the other cheek.

"See, if I had gone back to Bobby, none of this would be happening," Rachel bemoaned.

Twyla wasn't buying that. "Your wanting Bobby is why you're in this mess in the first place."

"I can't help it. Bobby still wanted me even though he married Shante," Rachel said defensively.

"Yeah, but you married Lester, which should've put an end to your pining after Bobby. And after all that mess you did trying to get him back and the fact that you almost broke up his and Shante's wedding, well, you can understand why Shante wanted to pay you back."

She was retelling the story in a way Rachel didn't want to hear. "Whose side are you on?"

"Yours, of course. But I'm just saying, don't even start thinking about Bobby. He and Shante are divorced. He's back in the military, off fighting in this stupid war. She's off somewhere probably drowning her sorrows in a carton of Ben & Jerry's." Rachel couldn't help but smile at Twyla's quip about Shante's weight. "And you have moved on with your life," Twyla declared.

"That's just it. How am I supposed to move on with this trick constantly coming around to cause me grief? If this baby turns out to be Lester's . . ." Rachel let her words trail off. She didn't even want to think about that.

"Just relax. Try to stay positive that everything will work out." Twyla counted off the next three steps on her fingers. "Mary will have her little crumbsnatcher. You'll find out it's not Lester's. She'll move away and everyone will live happily ever after."

Rachel turned up her lips. How she wished she could believe that. The feeling raging in her gut, though, told her this couldn't possibly end that easily.

Chapter 4

Jonathan Jackson couldn't stop staring at his son. Chase was growing into a handsome young man. At eight, he was the spitting image of his mother, Angela, but he definitely had Jonathan's smile.

Over the last few months, their relationship had really flourished and Jonathan couldn't be happier. He loved his new job as a high school counselor, and he loved spending time with his son. Chase was starting to ask a lot of uncomfortable questions, though—like the one he was asking right now.

"Dad, are you going to answer me?" Chase asked.

"I'm sorry, son. What did you say?" Jonathan said, trying to buy time to gather his thoughts.

Chase sighed like he hated repeating himself. "I said, when are you going to get remarried? My friend Justin's dad just remarried this thirty-year-old woman, and for an old lady, she's hot."

Amused, Jonathan ruffled his son's curly hair. "What do you know about hot? And, wait a minute. I'm thirty-four, so what does that make me?"

"You're ancient," Chase joked.

Jonathan playfully jumped on his son and wrestled him to the floor. Chase giggled with merriment.

When Jonathan finally let him be, Chase picked up where he'd left off. "I'm just saying. Mom's remarried. I think it's okay if you do it, too."

That thought still tripped a small pang in Jonathan's heart. He had expected that Angela would get remarried, and, in fact, he was happy that she had found happiness—especially considering the way that he had hurt her. He just hadn't expected it to happen so soon. She and Steve had become engaged, then married, in a matter of months.

Jonathan's mood grew solemn as he thought back to those early days, when he'd refused to accept that he was gay. He had met and fallen in love with a guy named Tracy when he'd gone away to college in Atlanta, but he'd kept that relationship hidden, especially from his father. When he'd graduated, he'd moved back home with the hope of forgetting that lifestyle and living the life he was expected to live—the pastor of Zion Hill, married to his high school sweetheart, Angela.

Jonathan had truly thought that he could let his past die. He'd thought that he could live up to what everyone else expected of him and live his life as a straight man. But Tracy had made it nearly impossible. He hadn't wanted to let Jonathan go. Angela had come home six months after they'd married—when she'd been eight months pregnant—and picked up the telephone to overhear a heated, love-laced conversation between Jonathan and Tracy. Jonathan's heart had dropped into his stomach when he'd realized Angela had been on the other line, listening in. Naturally, she'd gone ballistic and thrown him out. Her family had been livid. They were longtime, upstanding members of Zion Hill, and to have their only daughter humiliated and hurt like that caused them immeasurable pain.

That's why Jonathan couldn't blame Angela for not wanting him around Chase, even though her rationale that his "gayness might rub off" on her son was crazy. He'd tried to be understanding when she'd taken Chase and moved from Houston to Milwaukee, and he'd given her space. But the ache in his heart had soon become too much to bear, and he'd sued for joint custody.

Things had gotten real ugly for a minute, but eventually they'd managed to reach a peaceful accord. He'd promised not to bring his lifestyle around their child, and Angela had promised to stop fighting his being a part of Chase's life.

Jonathan had been ecstatic when Angela and Chase had moved back to Houston. Although he hated the forty-five-minute drive across town to see his son, Jonathan was grateful that Angela had moved to Spring, a suburb on the north side of Houston. Chase was living in a totally different environment, away from people who might know Jonathan's history and, in turn, tease the little boy about his dad. That was something Jonathan never, ever wanted. It was why he'd made up in his mind that his son would come first. There would be no serious relationships. That didn't mean he didn't have urges and needs, and he did go out on occasional dates, but he told himself that until Chase was old enough to understand, he would know nothing about his father's lifestyle. Right now Chase was his priority.

". . . I mean, Daddy, Steve is cool and all," Chase continued, snapping Jonathan back to their conversation. Angela's new husband was an investment banker who didn't really care for Jonathan but tried to keep the peace for Angela's sake. "But I think it would be cool to have a stepmom, too, especially if she's hot."

"Boy, stop talking about somebody being hot. You're too young to know anything about someone being hot," Jonathan chastised as he picked up the PlayStation's controller and handed it to his son.

Chase took the controller. "Uh-uh. Mama lets me have a girlfriend."

Jonathan spun his head toward his son. "What?"

"I have a girlfriend. In fact, I have two of them. Mama said I can have as many girlfriends as I want."

"Son, you are too young to be thinking about girls," Jonathan said. His heart felt heavy. He couldn't believe Angela would even entertain the idea of an eight-year-old having a girlfriend. Then again, she was probably pushing Chase at girls so early because of him.

"So, what about it?" Chase asked.

"What about what?" Jonathan replied.

"What about you getting married?"

"Son, I'll tell you what. Let me worry about when I get married, and you worry about doing well in school. Better yet, how about you worry about this butt-whipping I'm about to give you on this PlayStation game?" He pushed the Play button on the unit.

"In your dreams, Dad," Chase said, shifting the wireless controller in his hands. "I'm here for the whole spring break week, and I'm gonna beat you every day at a different game."

"Bring it on, buddy!"

They battled for a few minutes before the doorbell rang. Jonathan glanced toward the door.

"Take that," Chase said, his warrior knocking Jonathan's warrior off his post.

"No fair," Jonathan said, pulling himself up off the floor. "I was distracted."

"Yeah, boy!" Chase stood up and danced on top of the ottoman. "Don't make excuses. I beat you, I beat you!"

Jonathan laughed as he watched his son's clumsy dance. Chase might've gotten his looks from his mother, but he definitely got his lack of rhythm from Jonathan.

"Hey, baby sister," Jonathan said when he opened the door and saw Rachel standing there.

"Hey, big bro." Rachel kissed her brother on the cheek and walked into the living room. Chase jumped off the ottoman and raced over and threw his arms around Rachel's wide belly.

"Auntie Rachel!" He pulled back and looked at her stomach with pop eyes. "Wow, you're bigger than a house."

"Chase! Be nice," Jonathan said.

"What?" he asked innocently. "She is."

Rachel laughed. "It's okay. He's right, Jonathan. I am big as a house." She rubbed her belly. "I am so ready for this baby to arrive." She plopped down on the sofa. "I was just on my way home and thought I would stop in and check on you and see my nephew."

"Well, you came right on time because I was just beating up on this little knucklehead on the PlayStation."

"No, he wasn't," Chase protested.

"Trust me, baby. I believe you," Rachel said, squeezing his chin.

"So, where's Jordan?" Chase asked. Even though Jordan was a few years older than Chase, the two had immediately clicked and become best buds over the last few months.

"He's at home."

"Awww, man, I wish you had brought him," Chase said.

"I'll make sure I do it next time."

"Do you want something to drink?" Jonathan asked.

"Yes," Rachel said, pulling herself up off the sofa and following her brother into the kitchen. "I'll take a margarita."

He cut his eyes and Rachel shrugged. "Man, nobody wants to cooperate with my drink requests."

Jonathan reached into the refrigerator and grabbed a bottled water. "You talked to Dad?"

Rachel took the water, twisted the top off, then took a swig.

"Yeah, I actually was going to run by there, but he told me Aunt Minnie was in town and I'm not in the mood to deal with her right now."

Jonathan groaned at the mention of his dad's older sister. She was a deeply religious woman who swore she was God's personal assistant. She was so overbearing, she even carried around holy water in her purse.

"I'm glad I didn't go by there then," Jonathan said. Even though their father had remarried, they still tried to check on him a couple of times a week. He had been diagnosed with prostate cancer, and after a phase of remission, it was back. The chemotherapy to battle it kept Simon sluggish and tired all the time. He didn't get out of the house much anymore, not even for church.

"Well, we've been summoned to dinner Sunday," Rachel announced to him.

"Thanks, but no thanks," Jonathan replied.

"I'm sorry, did you think that was a request?" She gave him a knowing look. "Well, it wasn't. Daddy wants all of us to come. David is bringing his new girlfriend. He said Brenda is fixing a big Sunday dinner, and Aunt Minnie is looking forward to seeing us all."

"Well, you guys enjoy. I won't be able to make it," Jonathan said flatly. On the list of things he wanted to do in his life, being around his aunt Minnie ranked right below a root canal. No, he'd pass on Aunt Minnie for now. But he knew before his aunt left town, she'd find her way to him—and give him grief about his lifestyle.

Chapter 5

Mary fluffed out the curls in her hair, surveyed the raspberry-colored peasant dress in the full-length mirror, and smiled. For a pregnant woman about to pop, she didn't look half-bad.

"I can't believe you're really going out with him," Bernice said. She'd been over at Mary's apartment for the past two hours. While she'd claimed she'd been in the area and had just wanted to stop by, Mary knew she was being nosy. She didn't blame her friend, though. She'd probably have done the same thing if the tables had been turned.

"Believe it." Mary laughed as she pulled out her lip gloss to add another coat. "It just happened. I met him at the convenience store near the church. He'd met me once before but he didn't remember it, so it's like we started fresh."

"So he asked you out?"

"Actually, he had his son with him. So I asked him to come over and help me put together my crib and well, let's just say, I took it from there." She puffed out her lips in a kiss. "We've been going out for three weeks now and I can tell you already, I have him wrapped around my finger."

"Dang, I don't understand how you can pull a man at nine months pregnant." Bernice shook her head in exasperation. "I can't get a man to look my way period."

"Stop exaggerating," Mary said. "First of all, I'm eight months. Secondly, you had a date last weekend."

"Yeah, with someone I met on Match.com. And he must've sent a photo from twenty years ago because he didn't look anything like it."

Mary laughed as she leaned in toward the mirror to apply her mascara. "Well, once I turned on the charm, he was immediately smitten."

"*Smitten*? Is that how you were talking?"

"Some guys do appreciate Southern charm."

"Whatever. All I know," Bernice said as she flipped through a *People* magazine, "is that when the shinola hits the fan, you make sure I have a front-row seat."

"Yeah, yeah, yeah," Mary said, reaching down and pulling the magazine out of Bernice's hand. She tossed it on the bed. "But right now you've got to go. He'll be here any minute and I don't want any distractions."

"Awww, man, why do I have to leave?" Bernice said, looking

around for her shoes, which she'd kicked off when she'd first arrived. "I want to meet him."

"Another time, another place," Mary said, scooting her toward the door.

"Fine," Bernice said as she grabbed her shoes. "But you make sure you call me tomorrow and tell me how it went. I don't know what kind of plan you have brewing, but I know it's got to be good."

"I will fill you in later. Bye." Mary pushed Bernice through the door and quickly closed it before her friend found more reasons to stay around.

Mary couldn't help but smile at how well this plan was coming together. This whole affair had started out as payback for Shante, the wife of Rachel's son's father, Bobby Clark. Shante despised Rachel and had hired Mary to seduce Lester. Only Mary had fallen head over heels for Lester. The trap had started out innocently enough, and it had just been another job to Mary. But Lester had treated her like she'd never been treated before. Considering her dysfunctional upbringing and the toxic relationship she'd just abandoned with her ex-boyfriend Craig, that had been a welcome feeling.

Lester had treated Mary with love and respect, something she'd never had growing up in Anniston, Alabama. He'd made her feel worthy, and that had made her love him even more. Mary was convinced that she and Lester would be living happily ever after if not for that Jezebel of a wife. Rachel not only didn't appreciate Lester, but she also didn't deserve his love.

31

So Mary had made it her life's mission to win Lester's heart for good. Lester was too honorable to leave Rachel, but Mary was confident that Rachel would leave him in a heartbeat—if Mary pushed the right buttons.

She patted her stomach. This was the biggest button of them all. She hadn't counted on Rachel being pregnant at the same time, but hey, that only added spice to the pot. And now this date, well, this was just extra seasoning to give it a little more kick.

Bernice hadn't been gone ten minutes when the doorbell rang. Mary took a deep breath and allowed it to ring one more time before walking over to it.

"Hi," she said, throwing the door open. "Don't you look handsome?"

"And so do you." He leaned in and kissed her on the cheek.

"Come on in."

He walked inside her apartment, a huge smile across his face.

"So, where's your son?" Mary asked.

"He's with my family. They were all too happy to babysit when they heard I had a date." He laughed.

"Well, I can't wait to meet them," Mary said.

"As a matter of fact, I'm glad you said that. How would you like to come to dinner on Sunday? You can meet my dad then. In fact, the whole family will be there."

Mary tried her best to contain the hilarious smile she felt inside. She had to be the luckiest woman in the world. David had told her all about his last girlfriend, Tawny. She'd been a drug addict who had been arrested for trying to kill Rachel (Mary couldn't blame her for that). After dealing with her, it was no wonder David considered Mary a prize—even at eight months pregnant.

"Of course I would love to come," Mary said, grabbing her purse. She draped her arm through his as he led her to the door. "Dinner on Sunday it is. I can't wait to meet the wonderful Rev. Simon Jackson. I would love to meet your whole family."

David squeezed his arm around her waist. "I'm sure my family would love to meet you."

Mary was on cloud nine. She hoped Lester would be at the dinner. Yeah, her fling with David would probably end after that, but she would have sent a message to Lester that she wasn't going anywhere and the sooner he realized that, the better off everyone would be. And hey, maybe she'd get lucky. Maybe her dating David would be the match that would make Rachel explode and leave Lester for good. Mary would be there to pick up the pieces, and she, Lester, and their child could live happily ever after.

Chapter 6

Rachel took a deep breath and pushed her dad's front door open.

"Hey, anybody home?" she called out as she made her way into the foyer. She still winced a little when she saw her dad's picture sitting in an eight-by-ten-inch frame with his new wife, Brenda, on the small table near the door. The first time Rachel had seen it, she'd flipped. This was her mother's home. Even though her mother had been dead for eight years, Rachel still didn't like the idea of Brenda trying to act like Loretta didn't exist. Instead of causing a scene, Brenda had taken the picture down—despite Simon's protests—and wouldn't put it back up until all three of the kids were comfortable.

After a year of Brenda's patiently bearing Rachel's sarcastic remarks, Rachel had resolved that it was okay for her father to move on. Brenda had tearfully told her she'd never wanted to take Loretta's place, but she did want to make Simon happy. From that day on, Rachel had been close to Brenda. She told her father that since her mother wasn't around to make him happy, Brenda was exactly the type of woman she'd choose to do it instead.

"Well, hallelujah and praise Jesus," Aunt Minnie said, meeting Rachel in the doorway to the kitchen. She was a robust woman, with long graying hair that hung down her back. She had her brother's caramel coloring and actually looked like Simon with a wig on. She wore a homemade baby blue dress with a white lace collar and some white nurse shoes. "It's so wonderful to see my favorite niece." Minnie reached out to hug Rachel.

Rachel ignored the "favorite niece" comment, seeing as how she was Minnie's only niece. "Hi, Aunt Minnie." She gave her aunt a hug. It was a respectful hug, not an I'm-happy-to-see-you hug. Aunt Minnie, her father's oldest sister, usually stirred up a lot of family drama because she stood in judgment of everything and everybody.

Minnie squeezed Rachel tightly, then pulled back and surveyed her appearance. "Look at you, looking like you 'bout to pop." She rubbed Rachel's belly. "Hey, sugar plum, it's your great-aunt Minnie," she said, leaning down and talking to Rachel's stomach. "Are you nice and warm in there? Is your mama feeding you all of your nutrients? You let your auntie know if your mama ain't treating you right." She looked over at Nia and Jordan, who were both standing behind Rachel like the plump old woman scared them. "And look at you two." She yanked them both from behind Rachel and gave them bear hugs. "I ain't seen you since you two were knee high to a pup."

"Ewww," Jordan said, trying to squeeze out of her embrace.

As soon as she released them, both kids took off running to the den. Minnie smiled as she watched them dart off.

"Where's the good reverend?" she asked, turning back to Rachel.

"He had an emergency at the church. So, how have you been?" Rachel asked before her aunt could start bombarding her with more questions.

Minnie put her hands on her hips and chuckled. "Any day the good Lord sees fit to wake me up is a good day."

Rachel smiled patiently, not replying. She'd learned a long time ago that unless she wanted a six-hour lesson on the Bible, she should not engage her aunt in any discussion of religion.

"Well, where is everyone?" Rachel asked, changing the subject.

"They in the back, in the den." Minnie leaned in and lowered her voice. "I'm not sure about this young gal your daddy married. She look like she used to be kinda loose."

Rachel let out a sigh. "Brenda is a good woman. And more important, she's good for Dad." She didn't even touch the "young" comment, since Brenda was a year older than Simon.

"Umph. We'll see." A smile returned to Minnie's face. "Girl, you look good. A First Lady? Umph! I'm just so happy to see that God exorcised those demons from your soul, because you were locked, stocked and bound for hell."

Rachel didn't know how to respond to that. She glanced around, looking for rescue. "Well, guess I'll go on back."

She quickly headed toward the den. Her father was sitting in his oversized recliner. Brenda sat across from him reading a Beverly Jenkins novel.

"Hey, Brenda. Hey, Daddy." Rachel walked over and kissed her father on the head. His salt-and-pepper hair was now all salt. He looked like he'd aged ten years in just the past year.

"Hey, baby girl."

"How are you feeling today?" she asked, assessing him.

"I'm feeling mighty good today, except for that." He pointed toward the TV. "Why your kids come in here trying to change my TV?"

"'Cause you're always watching this show with the man that don't comb his hair," Nia whined. Rachel knew she was talking about *Sanford and Son,* her father's favorite show. "And I wanna watch *Hannah Montana.*"

"Hannah who?"

"Nobody, Dad," Rachel said. "Kids, go watch TV upstairs until dinner is ready."

Rachel expected them to protest, but they gave their grandfather a lot more respect than they gave their parents. They both raced up the stairs, no doubt trying to be the first one to reach the TV clicker up there.

A buzzer went off in the kitchen and Brenda stood. "That's my cue. Dinner will be ready in a minute."

"Do you need help with anything?" Rachel asked.

"No, thanks, I got it." Brenda disappeared into the kitchen.

"Where is Jonathan and David?" Minnie asked as she came in and sat on the sofa across from Simon.

Rachel noticed her father suddenly turn all of his attention to the TV. That told her Jonathan wasn't coming.

"Jon's not going, umm, he's not going to be able to make it," Rachel stammered when it was obvious her father wasn't going to help. She wasn't completely lying about Jon. She just left out the part about him not *wanting* to make it. "And David said he'll be late because he had to work."

Thankfully, Brenda stuck her head back in and announced that dinner was ready, so Rachel didn't have to go into detail.

Rachel got the kids back down to the dinner table, and after Simon said grace, they all dug into the hearty meal of fried chicken, collard greens, hot water cornbread, sweet potatoes, dirty rice and peach cobbler.

"So," Minnie began after a round of small talk, "why couldn't Jonathan make it?"

Simon promptly stuck a forkful of greens into his mouth. Rachel cut her eyes at her father and said, "He just had something to do."

"Umph," Minnie said. "Has he rebuked that gay devil in him?"

"Minnie!" Simon said despite his mouthful of food. He shot his sister a stern look.

"What?" she asked too innocently.

Simon took his napkin and dabbed the corner of his mouth as he swallowed. "I'm gonna need you not to go there."

She shook her head, ready as always to do battle for the

Lord. "I just don't understand how we're supposed to sit around and act like this is okay." She looked around the table. "Does anybody but me know that homosexuality is a sin?"

"So is lying. So is fornicating—and Lord knows you did enough of that back in your day," Simon snapped.

Minnie's hand went to her chest as an appalled expression blanketed her face.

Simon caught himself, realizing the kids were sitting there. He turned to them and said, "Jordan, Nia, go finish your food on the patio."

They knew the situation was serious because neither said a word as they gathered up their plates.

"Now, Minnie, I've been letting you be you since you got here," Simon said as soon as the children were gone. His voice had taken on a force Rachel hadn't seen in a while. "But I'm not going to let you come in my house and disrespect my son."

Minnie folded her arms across her chest and glared at her brother. "How can you call yourself a man of God, then condone his behavior?"

"I don't condone anything," Simon said. "I don't like it one bit and I wish that it were not the case. I have prayed around the clock for God to deliver my child, but in the end, that's between Jonathan and God. I don't want any man to judge me, so I'm not going to judge him. And just like I hope God forgives me for my sins, I hope He can forgive Jonathan for his."

"So, you just think it's okay for a pastor to have a funny son?" she asked.

"I actually like his sense of humor," Simon quipped.

"You know what I mean," she huffed.

Simon took a deep breath. "Of course I don't think it's okay. I struggle with it on a daily basis, but he's still my son and just because you love the sinner doesn't mean you like the sin."

"I don't care what you say, it ain't right. It's an abomination!" she said, slamming her hands down on the dining room table.

Simon didn't back down one bit. "How you gon' stand in judgment of my children when both of your sons are in prison?"

"Least they ain't funny," she proclaimed.

"You don't know what they're doing in prison," Simon growled. "They may have their own boyfriends."

"Or be somebody's boy toy," Rachel threw in, not exactly a wallflower in the family battles herself.

Minnie looked horrified.

"Can we find something else to talk about?" Brenda finally interjected.

Minnie cocked her head and said spitefully, "So, is David still on crack?"

"Minnie," Simon said sternly, shaking his fork her way, "you got one more time and I'm going to ask you to leave my house—sister or not."

"Fine!" Minnie threw up her hands. "Don't wanna talk about your gay son. Don't wanna talk about your crackhead son." She motioned toward Rachel. "And I'm sure we can't even touch the two kids this one had 'fo' she was even legal."

"Excuse me?" Rachel said. "How did this become about me?"

Minnie ignored her and turned to Brenda. "So what do you

41

think about the war in Afghanistan? Or the rising price of gas? Is that more suitable conversation?" She didn't wait on an answer. "Let's just ignore the elephant in the room and talk about the price of gas, or where the next Olympics should be held."

Rachel sighed heavily. Jonathan had been right to pass on this dinner. She was trying to figure out how she could make an early exit when David appeared in the dining room doorway. He was holding his nine-month-old son, DJ, in his arms.

"Hey, hey, hey. I know my lovely family ain't up in here fighting," he joked.

"You're late," Simon said, standing to greet his son. He seemed grateful for the interruption. "And give me my grandson," he said, taking DJ from David. David had planned to fight for permanent custody of DJ, but since Tawny, DJ's mother, had been arrested for trying to run Rachel over, he hadn't had to.

"Hey, Aunt Minnie." David walked over and gave her a hug. "What's up, Rach?" He tousled her hair. "Sorry I was late. I had to work, then run by and pick up my girlfriend."

"Girlfriend," Aunt Minnie said. "You hear that, Simon. David brought his *girlfriend*."

"Minnie . . . ," Simon said.

She feigned innocence before turning her attention back to David. "Where is she?"

"She had to go to the restroom." He gave Rachel a wink. "She's pregnant like you. We can't go ten minutes without her having to pee."

"Pregnant?" Simon said, his eyes wide.

"Don't worry, Dad, it's not mine. She was pregnant when I met her, but her baby's father abandoned her." He shrugged, trying to explain. "We just hit it off. I really like her, and if she doesn't have a problem with my kid, I don't have a problem with hers."

"Well, how noble, son," Simon said proudly. "I can't wait to meet the woman that has you floating around on cloud nine."

"Me either," Rachel replied.

She was very happy to see her brother clean and sober and far, far away from his psychotic ex-girlfriend Tawny. She was the one who had kept David hooked on drugs. He'd been clean since their mother's death. And anyone who could help him stay that way was worth having around.

"Well, who knows, she might be the one," Simon said.

"We haven't been going out that long, so I think Dad is jumping ahead of himself," David cautioned. "But I am feeling her."

"And I'm feeling you, too."

They all turned toward the woman who appeared in the entryway to the dining room. Rachel's mouth dropped open. Simon bolted to his feet.

"What in the world is going on?" Simon said, immediately handing DJ to Brenda.

David was baffled as he looked back and forth between Rachel, who was glaring at his girlfriend, and the look of shock on Simon's and Brenda's faces.

"What do you mean, what's going on?" David asked.

"What the hell are you doing here?" Rachel asked.

"I'm here with David," Mary said innocently.

David jerked about. "Do you know her?" he asked his sister.

Rachel responded wearily, "David, I know you work on Sundays and never go to church, but do you have any idea who this is?"

"Yes, she's my new girlfriend." He looked around the room again, taking in all the shocked expressions. "Does someone want to tell me what's going on?"

"Yeah, me, too," Minnie chimed in.

Rachel didn't take her eyes off Mary as she said, "David, you know all the drama I've been going through with Lester?"

"Yeah, *and* . . . ?"

"This is the home wrecker that's responsible."

David stepped back, a look of shock on his face. "Th-this is *your* Mary?" he stammered.

Mary reached out for his hand. "No, David, I'm *your* Mary."

He yanked his hand back. "What is going on? Did you know who I was?"

"Of course she did," Rachel spat, shooting Mary daggers. "She's using you to mess with me."

David stared at Mary with a disgusted kind of awe. "Are you trying to play some kind of sick game with me?"

"David, sweetheart, don't be like that."

"Young lady, I don't know what type of game you're trying to play with my family," Simon said, waving his finger at her, "but I can tell you right now, I do not appreciate you coming into my home."

"Rev. Jackson, I—"

He held his hand up to cut her off. "Save it. I'm going to ask you one time to get out of my house, while you still can." He glanced over at Rachel, whose hand had slowly made its way to a steak knife. She was gripping it firmly as she slowly rocked back and forth. "Or I cannot be responsible for what my daughter does."

Minnie continued looking back and forth like she was in the middle of a good movie.

Mary let out a frustrated sigh. "Fine." She looked at David. "David?"

"You need to go," he said sternly. He looked like it was taking everything in his power to contain his anger.

"How am I supposed to get home?"

"I will have a cab come pick you up out front. Now please get out of my house," Simon said.

Mary eyed the knife, which Rachel was now digging into the table. "Fine." She spun around and walked out.

The room remained silent for a full minute after she left. Finally, Minnie spoke.

"Oooo-wee. It looks like I got here just in time. Thank you, Jesus." She piled some more greens on her plate. "Because this family sho' is in shambles. But don't you all worry. Aunt Minnie's going to get y'all back on the right track. Guess now's as good a time as any to tell you I'm here to stay for a while. My good friend, Lillie Mae, is undergoing chemotherapy at MD Anderson. The good Lord sho' know what He doin'."

"Rachel, I'm sorry, I didn't know," David said, ignoring his aunt's announcement.

Rachel couldn't respond as she scooted back from the table. Her hands were shaking. First the church, now this woman had the audacity to show up at her father's home? This was too much to bear.

"Rachel," David called out as she took off.

"Son, let her go," Rachel heard her father say. "You know she needs to be by herself when she's upset."

Rachel didn't hear the rest of the conversation. She was already out the door and heading to her car. She'd come back to pick up the kids after she cooled off. She had to get out of this house. She was about to lose it, and everything that she'd ever worked for—her family, her status in the church, her growth as a Christian—would be in vain.

Anger clouded her vision as she backed out of her father's driveway, and Rachel couldn't help but wonder if getting even with Mary would be worth losing it all. The way she was feeling right now, it just might be.

Chapter 7

"Hey, handsome," Mary said as she opened the front door to her apartment. "I'm so glad you came over." She had been pleasantly surprised when David had called and said he was on his way over. He'd still been angry, but the fact that he'd called her before the night was over and told her he was coming by spoke volumes.

"I don't want you to be mad," she purred. She was wearing a long, sexy nightgown cut low in the front. Her pregnancy had made her full breasts even more plump, and she wasn't hesitating to flaunt them.

David pushed past her and into her living room. "Oh, I'm about six blocks past mad. I just came here because I'm trying to understand what type of game you're playing."

She closed the door and followed him into the front room. "What do you mean, David?"

He spun toward her, his eyes blazing. "Was this all part of some elaborate plan? You hadn't caused my sister enough grief, so you were going to infiltrate my life? For what, to get close to Lester? To hurt Rachel? Was everything carefully orchestrated to bring pain to my family?"

His words were laced with anger. Mary knew David definitely liked her. Had from the first moment they'd met. And while their affair had escalated quickly, she'd known that she had him wrapped around her finger from the moment she'd pleasured him and he'd almost lost his mind. She just needed to tap into that part of him right now.

On the other hand, the sight of Rachel's face today was all the satisfaction she'd wanted. So, really, she was okay with David letting her go.

"David, contrary to your belief, I didn't come after you." Technically, she was telling the truth. Their meeting had been purely coincidental. Yet she'd known who he was immediately, and she'd assumed he'd known who she was. But the longer they'd talked, the more she'd realized that he hadn't had a clue. On the spur of the moment, she'd decided to ask him over to help her put together her baby crib. They'd laughed and had a great time, and the next thing she'd known, he'd been asking her out.

That had been only a month ago. While Mary had felt bad initially about using David, she'd told herself that it was divine intervention to get back at Lester.

"Just tell me this, Mary," he said. "Have you known from the beginning who I was?"

She rolled her eyes but didn't answer.

"You knew?" he replied like he was hoping for a different answer. "So all along it was some kind of plot to snag me and harm my family?"

"I hate to burst your bubble," she said with an attitude, "but you, a reformed crackhead, and your equally messed-up family really aren't that important." She closed her eyes to calm herself. "I'm sorry, that was uncalled for." She blew a frustrated breath. "I really like you, and I hate how you're coming over here accusing me of stuff. There was no plot," she lied as she pointed to her stomach. "In case you hadn't noticed, not many men will try to talk to me. And I found someone who liked me in spite of being pregnant, and that's all that mattered."

He looked like he was weighing her words. "So how long did you think you were going to play all of this out?"

She shrugged. "I didn't think. I just took it day by day." That part was the truth. She hadn't thought past causing Rachel pain. Yeah, she liked hanging out with David, but there was no attraction.

"I just don't believe this." David rubbed his hands over his head.

"Look," Mary said, taking a step toward him. "This doesn't have to be over. I know it may be a little difficult—"

"Are you serious?" he said, backing up from her like she was a snake. "You're lucky I turned my life around, because the old

49

David—the crackhead David, as you say—would be whoopin' your ass right now."

Mary's eyes widened in shock.

David continued looking at her in disgust. "I just came over here to tell you that we may seem dysfunctional, but at the end of the day, family is what's most important. Now, I know you don't know anything about that," he stressed.

That hurt, and David knew it. She had shared with him her horrible childhood growing up in foster care. She'd been the product of a one-night stand, and her stripper mother had had no interest in being a mother, so when Mary was age seven, after years of neglect, the state had stepped in and removed her. She'd immediately been placed in foster care and kept moving. Screw all those stories about cute white babies being in high demand. Nobody had wanted her, and the few times she'd thought she was about to get a family, some pervert—the father, an uncle—would cross the line and she'd rebel and they'd send her right back to the foster home.

"Do you understand me?" David said, interrupting her thoughts. He'd lowered his voice. "Try me again, Mary, and I promise you, you'll live to regret it. Stay the hell away from me and my family."

He turned and stormed out, not giving her a chance to reply.

Chapter 8

Jonathan had never seen someone so troubled. He sat across from the student, who looked like he carried the weight of someone much older than fifteen.

"So, Roderick, you wanna tell me what's really going on?" Jonathan asked as he leaned forward on his desk.

Roderick was a demure boy who never smiled. He lived in the shadow of his twin brother, Rodney, a superstar athlete at Spring High School, where Jonathan worked as an academic counselor.

"N-nothing's going on, Mr. Jackson," Roderick said.

"Yes, it is," Jonathan replied. He walked around his desk, shut his office door, then took a seat in the chair next to Roderick. "Mrs. Abrams referred you to me and said she was really concerned about you. Your grades are dropping, she says you're withdrawn, and you haven't turned in your last three assignments."

Roderick shrugged, but it was obvious that something was weighing on him.

"Does this have anything to do with Rodney's fight yesterday?" Jonathan asked.

Roderick lowered his eyes and didn't respond.

"Mrs. Abrams said Rodney started the fight. You know this could jeopardize his football scholarship?" Jonathan continued.

That was the catalyst to open the floodgates. Roderick started crying. "It's not fair," he said. "Rodney was defending me. He's always defending me."

Jonathan knew Roderick was picked on a lot. Unlike his athletic brother, Roderick had effeminate ways that garnered teasing from all the boys at school.

"Why do you need defending?" Jonathan gently asked.

"Because they're always messing with me, calling me names, like fag and booty bumper. I'm not gay," he protested.

The words made Jonathan cringe, and his heart went out to the young boy. He didn't know whether Roderick was gay or not, but he knew the turmoil the boy must have been feeling.

"Just 'cause I'm not all macho like my brother, they wanna harass me!"

"Well, how did the fight start?" Jonathan asked.

"Marcus Washington said he saw me kiss Benjamin Morris behind the gym, but he's lying. We were talking about some art stuff. Ben is my friend. We didn't do anything, but Marcus told everybody that we did and Rodney got mad. He told

Marcus to shut up and Marcus just kept on, and that's when my brother punched him." Roderick buried his head in his hands and began sobbing. "I didn't do anything," he cried over and over. "I don't want my brother losing his scholarship because of me. He's already always in trouble. My dad's gonna kill me."

Jon reached over and gently rubbed Roderick's back. He so felt the boy's pain, especially because he knew Benjamin Morris was flamboyantly gay. Anyone that hung with him was subject to teasing. Benjamin didn't care what others said about him, but those who chose to be friends with him did.

"Shhh, it's going to be all right," Jonathan said soothingly.

Just then Jonathan's door burst open. "Get your nasty hands off my son!" Jonathan's eyes shot toward the man standing in his doorway, looking like a linebacker for the Oakland Raiders. He had to be six-three, three hundred fifty pounds, and he had a wide nose and square chin, just like his twin boys.

"Dad!" Roderick jumped up instinctively and stepped behind Jonathan.

"Boy, get your butt over here!"

Jonathan rose as well. "Mr. Hurst, I was just—"

"I see what you were just doing. It's a damn shame they let people like you work with these boys."

Jonathan narrowed his eyes. "Excuse me? People like me? What does that mean?"

Mr. Hurst reached behind Jonathan and snatched Roderick so hard that the boy fell to the floor. He let out a small yelp as he fell.

"Get your sissy ass up, boy," Mr. Hurst bellowed.

Roderick fought back his tears as he struggled to stand up.

"Mr. Hurst! I will not allow you to manhandle this boy," Jonathan said.

Mr. Hurst stepped in Jonathan's face. He towered above Jonathan, and while Jonathan was scared, he refused to back down.

"You don't tell me how to handle my son," Mr. Hurst snarled. "I know all about you. I know someone from your church, so I know what kind of man you are. You probably sitting up here trying to convince my son that it's okay for him to be a sissy."

"Mr. Hurst, Roderick is not a sissy. He's a good young boy who—"

"Who needs to man up!"

Roderick was literally shaking in his shoes, and Jonathan knew he had to try and calm Mr. Hurst down.

"Mr. Hurst, the real concern is Rodney's fighting. He started the fight—"

"He shoulda broke their legs."

"Mr. Hurst," Jonathan continued, "both of your sons are good kids, but Rodney's constant fighting may cause him to lose his football scholarship. Is that what you want?"

That hit home, because he finally settled down.

"My boy is going to college," Mr. Hurst said, a lot more calmly.

"Not if he doesn't stop fighting. He might not even be graduating if he doesn't get his temper under control."

Mr. Hurst glared at Roderick. "He keeps fighting because of this boy." He grabbed Roderick's arm and shook him. "He can't stand up for himself. And then that swishing way he walks just opens the door for folks to give him a hard time."

That caused Roderick to tear up again. Mr. Hurst slapped him upside the back of his head, and Roderick cried even harder.

"Mr. Hurst! Please don't do that," Jonathan said.

"You see what I mean? Rodney would never stand up here and cry like no sissy."

Roderick didn't say a word. Sadly, Jonathan guessed, this was the treatment that he was used to.

"Mr. Hurst, there are some fundamental issues that I think we need to address," Jonathan began.

"I think you need to get me someone else in here to talk to because I don't want to talk to you."

"This is my job."

"I don't care what your job is. I don't want you talking to me or my sons. I don't want none of you rubbing off on them. Now, I'm going to make this boy a man if it's the last thing I do," he said, pointing to a shivering Roderick. "And I don't need you putting no 'just be you' foolish thoughts into his mind, do you hear me?"

"But—"

"Do you hear me?" he bellowed. "Now, get me a real man to talk to about my kids!"

Jonathan contemplated trying to say more, but he'd met men like Mr. Hurst—stubborn, obnoxious men who, no matter what anyone said, would never see anyone's way but their own.

"Fine," Jonathan said, exiting his office. As soon as the door closed, he heard Mr. Hurst light into Roderick. Jonathan took a deep breath. He didn't know whether Roderick was gay or not, and he didn't think Roderick knew. But if he was, Jonathan knew Roderick would never admit it. And as Jonathan listened to Mr. Hurst loudly go off, he couldn't help but wonder how anyone would think a person would *choose* to subject themselves to this torment.

Chapter 9

Today was a good day. In the past week since the dinner fiasco Rachel had managed to get over her anger. Initially, she'd thought maybe Mary's involvement with David meant she was giving up on Lester, but Rachel's gut told her that wasn't the case. She knew that woman, and David was just another tool she had used to make life miserable for Rachel. After a very long prayer, Rachel was refreshed. She convinced herself not to give Mary the satisfaction of making her life any more chaotic than it already was.

Rachel found herself humming an old gospel song as she folded up clothes that had been sitting in the dryer for the last three days. She'd had a peaceful night for a change, and Lester had been pleasantly surprised to wake up to find her cooking breakfast. She had greeted him with a smile, determined to take Twyla's advice and stay positive. Her change in attitude worked wonders. She didn't cringe when he kissed her neck, and he seized the opportunity. He spent all day rubbing her belly, massaging her neck and reminding her of how much he loved her. For once Mary didn't invade her thoughts. She imagined that her marriage was back to the way that it once was.

"Hey, babe," she said when Lester descended the stairway.

"Wow, lunch too? Clean clothes?" He laughed as he pointed toward the folded laundry. "I've died and gone to Heaven."

"Oh, you got jokes," Rachel replied, walking over and hugging him gently. She could feel the relief escape his body as he hugged her tightly in return. She closed her eyes and inhaled, grateful for moments like this—when she remembered just how much she loved her husband. If only she could have more of those. "Where are you going?" Rachel pulled herself away from his grip and he smiled happily as she motioned toward his velour jogging suit. "Even better, where are you going looking like my daddy? Can you get a nylon suit, please?"

He laughed as he rubbed a swatch of velour the wrong way. "Don't hate. Your daddy's got good taste. I'm going to go and stop by the church, and then I'll go pick the kids up from your dad," he said. "I want us to come back and enjoy the night as a family, maybe watch a movie or something."

"That sounds great." Lester had just gathered his keys when Rachel handed him the towels. "Here, these go upstairs."

"Man, I knew I should've snuck out the back door," he joked as he turned to go up. Despite the drama they had been going through for the past few months, Rachel knew Lester was good for her. He always saw the best in her. Even when she'd been doing scandalous things as a teen, like getting pregnant so young, pining after Bobby, wreaking havoc on Shante, spending hours in the club and starting fights with folks—some of which had happened after she'd become First Lady—through all of that, Lester had stood by her side. It's why she had learned to love him. She'd learned long ago that while she wanted to love Bobby, she *needed* to love Lester.

Her warm thoughts were interrupted by the ringing telephone.

"Hello," Rachel said, nestling the cordless phone between her ear and shoulder as she picked up another stack of clothes.

"Put Lester on the phone."

The warm and fuzzy feeling she'd had just a minute ago evaporated. Rachel gripped the phone. *No, this heifer didn't.*

"What did you just say?" Rachel said.

"I didn't stutter," Mary snapped. "Put Lester on the phone."

"You have lost your ever-lovin' mind," Rachel hissed into the phone. "You are out of order for calling my house in the first place. And you must be on some strong drugs if you think you're going to call my house and talk to my husband."

"Okay, fine," Mary spat. "Tell my baby's daddy to meet me at Hermann Hospital because I'm having his baby tonight." She slammed the phone down before Rachel could say anything else.

"Any more trivial housework you'd like me to do before I leave?"

Rachel spun toward Lester, who was grinning like a Cheshire cat—until he noticed the angry expression on Rachel's face.

"Uh . . . who was that on the phone?" he asked, noticing it was gripped tightly in Rachel's hand.

Rachel's chest began heaving up and down as her nostrils flared. Before she knew what she was doing, she hurled the cordless phone across the room. Once again, Lester ducked just in time.

"It was your baby's mama!" she screamed. "She demanded that you get to the hospital so you two could deliver your child."

"Rachel . . ."

Rachel fought back tears. "I am at the edge, Lester," she said, breathing heavily. "The fact that that woman even thinks that she has the right to call this house . . ."

"Baby, I'm so sorry."

"I'm sick and tired of your apologies!" she yelled. "I'm sick of this mess you got us caught up in, and I'm sick of this bit—"

"Rachel!" Lester interrupted. "Calm down. This isn't good for the baby."

Rachel was in tears now. Her good day had been ruined once again by this monster. She rubbed her stomach. The baby had started tossing, no doubt sensing her stress. "You wanna know what's not good for my baby?" she calmly said. "It's not good that her mother has to wonder whether she'll have a little brother or sister born within days of her. How do you plan on explaining that to her? Huh? You wanna know what else is not good?" She pointed at her stomach. "It's not good that my baby's life has to be put in jeopardy because her mother is so damn stressed behind the woman her daddy cheated with."

Lester lowered his head in shame. "I'm so . . . What can I do?"

Rachel took a deep breath. He was right about one thing. She couldn't let him stress her to the point of going into labor. "Handle her, Lester. I don't care how. Just handle her now. Or I promise you, I will."

Rachel stomped past her husband. She didn't know if he was going to the hospital or not. She didn't care to know. All she cared about was Lester getting that tramp under control, because if she had to do it, it wouldn't be pretty.

Chapter 10

"I knew you'd come." Mary smiled at the sight of Lester standing in her hospital doorway. His eyes immediately went to her stomach. She knew he was expecting to see a baby nestled in a blanket or even a bunch of machines hooked up to her. Shoot, she'd thought she would be holding a baby, too. She'd been scared to death when she'd started having contractions this morning. She hadn't planned to call Lester's house, but he had changed his cell phone number and she'd been so scared of delivering her baby alone that she'd panicked. Besides, Lester was one of the good guys. She knew he wouldn't let her go through this by herself, no matter how mad he was.

"Mary, what's going on?" Lester asked as he eased into the room.

She was fully dressed and sitting on the edge of the bed.

She rubbed her stomach and smiled. "False labor." She laughed uneasily. "Can you believe it? Boy, if that pain wasn't the real thing, I can't imagine what the real deal will feel like."

Lester stared at her in disbelief. "I cannot believe you did this."

"What? You think I did this on purpose." She feigned an appalled look. Of course, she wasn't above doing something like faking labor, but she really had thought that she was in labor. "I would not check myself into a hospital if I didn't really think I was." She'd gotten her neighbor to drive her to the hospital, and the pain had been so intense that she'd been worried about having her baby in the neighbor's Ford Taurus.

Lester let out a defeated sigh. "Okay, fine, but Mary, I need you to understand that what happened between you and I was a huge mistake. My wife has forgiven me, God has forgiven me, and I need you to leave me and my family alone."

"How do you expect me to do that when we have a child to raise?" she asked. It pained her every time he tried to tell her what they had was over. It couldn't be over. Lester was everything she needed in a man, everything she had dreamed of all those days pining away in foster care. She could do without him being a preacher, but he was sweet, loving, stable, and handsome. Plus, she knew that his parents had left him money when they died several years ago, and his grandmother had recently passed, leaving Lester her money as well. So on top of everything else, Lester was loaded.

"Mary, if the baby is mine, I will do right by you and the child," Lester promised. Then his voice took on a more forceful tone. "But until we know that for sure, I need you to leave me alone, and do not disrespect my wife by calling our home, do not disrespect her in our church, do not disrespect her, period."

Mary rolled her eyes. She could not for the life of her see what Lester saw in that woman. Why was he coming to her defense?

"And I need to be clear on something else as well," he continued. He walked closer to her, his voice taking on a firmness she'd never heard before. "I am not leaving my wife. If this child turns out to be mine—"

"There is no if," she said bluntly.

"If and when this child turns out to be mine, I will do right by you, but that means Rachel will be a part of the baby's life as well."

Mary was shocked by the idea. "That woman will get nowhere near my child," she declared. Lester must have lost his mind. It would be a cold day in hell before she let Rachel anywhere near her child.

Lester backed away, his lips pursed like he knew there was no getting through to her.

"Just remember what I said, Mary. I mean it. Stop harassing my family."

Mary glared back as he left. He was trying to be forceful with her, but she knew him. He was weak when it came to women. That's why Rachel had run all over him in the first place. No, it wasn't over. She'd seduced Lester once, she'd do it again. She was confident that it was just a matter of time.

The first man she'd hooked up with had promised to take

her away from her shabby life. He'd had money, but he'd also felt like that money had given him carte blanche to slap her around whenever he'd felt like it. And she had too much spunk to let anybody put their hands on her, so she'd left him.

Then Craig had come along. Craig Musgrove was her heart. The one man who was in her blood. She loved him with all of her heart, and in the beginning, he'd been her knight in shining armor. He'd dabbled in drugs, selling heroin and weed, nothing major. But he was a con artist to the tenth degree. For a while, it hadn't bothered Mary, but then he'd started involving her in his schemes, and she'd found herself doing things she'd never thought she'd do. The final straw had come when he'd killed someone. That had been more than she could handle. She'd moved on, and last she'd heard, Craig had run off and married some rich widow in North Carolina.

Mary shook off her thoughts of Craig. That was her past. Lester was her future. Now she just needed to figure out a way to make him realize that.

Chapter 11

Rachel inhaled deeply, struggling to maintain her cool. God had to be testing her. Seeing just how much she could take without acting a fool. Well, this was one test she was definitely about to flunk.

"She really doesn't know who she's messing with," Rachel overheard Mary saying. "I've only just begun."

She'd stumbled upon this conversation between Mary and Shante. Just the sound of Mary's voice made her skin crawl, but Shante didn't even go to Zion Hill anymore, so Rachel didn't know why she was here. No doubt just to be messy.

Twyla, who'd walked into church with Rachel, instinctively put her hand on her arm. "Rachel, let it go. This isn't the time or place." She pointed behind them. "And your kids are here."

They had just arrived at the church and were walking

around to the choir room when they heard Mary and Shante deep in conversation.

"I told you she wasn't nothing but a tramp," Shante said. "Me and Bobby would be together right now if it weren't for her stank behind, trying to act all high and mighty. I hope you take that heifer down."

"Oh, believe that," Mary replied. "I guarantee you, before my baby sees his first birthday, me and Lester will be together."

"No, I've had enough," Rachel growled, her chest heaving up and down.

Twyla gripped her friend's arm tighter. "The kids . . ."

Rachel looked back at Jordan, who was sitting on a bench engrossed in his Nintendo DS. Nia was playing with the belt on her skirt. They were oblivious to the drama that was unfolding around them.

Rachel didn't reply. She began removing her earrings. "I can't take this anymore. We can work all this out with the kids in therapy later."

Rachel stuffed the earrings in her purse as she rounded the corner. "Did I hear someone talking about me?"

Both Mary and Shante looked surprised, then a smirk crossed their faces.

"We may have been talking *about* you, but I don't think anyone was talking *to* you," Shante said.

Rachel glared at her. "How's Bobby? Oh, I'm sorry, you wouldn't know, since he left you. I'll see how he is when he calls tonight."

Shante seethed in anger. Rachel knew that would piss her

off. The last time they'd talked, Bobby had told her how Shante was blowing up his phone and email, but he wouldn't answer. Rachel turned away. After all, her battle wasn't with Shante. It was with the tramp standing directly in her face.

"Look, I have been as nice as possible in putting up with your conniving ways," Rachel said, stepping closer to Mary.

Mary put up a false bravado as she remarked to Shante, "Talk about the pot calling the kettle black." Her hands went to her hips. "Conniving? Aren't you the same woman who slashed Shante's tires, had her electricity cut off and, oh yeah, tried to steal her husband while you were married to some-one else?" Mary looked Rachel in the eye. "The bottom line, Madam First Lady, is that your beef needs to be with your hus-band. I did not hold a gun to his head and make him sleep with me. He was neglected, lonely and fed up with trying to make you love him." She laughed, like Rachel was stupid. "Didn't your mama ever teach you that what you won't do for your man, another woman will?"

Rachel felt a wave of fury consume her. "I would strongly suggest that you find a new church home," she slowly said.

"Or what?" Mary said defiantly.

Rachel could no longer contain herself. She reached back and slapped Mary as hard as she could. Stunned, Mary screamed and grabbed her cheek.

Twyla immediately jumped in front of Rachel and pushed her back. "Rachel! No!"

Before Rachel could act, Mary came charging at her. She pushed Rachel hard into the wall, and Twyla tumbled to the floor. Rachel screamed and grabbed Mary's hair, and flung her into the wall.

"Mommy!" Nia shouted.

Both Twyla and Shante struggled to pull them apart as a couple of deacons came rushing down the hallway.

"Have you two lost your minds?" Deacon Baker cried as another deacon succeeded in helping Twyla pull Rachel off Mary.

"Naw, let me at her!" Rachel said, kicking and screaming. She knew she had turned into a lunatic, but it was like she was having an out-of-body experience. "I need to beat this ho down!"

"Oh, that's real First Lady–like," Mary said, panting, as she pulled herself up off the floor.

Several people had started to gather in the hallway. One of the elders of the church. Sister Ida Hicks, stepped into the middle of the commotion.

"Lord, have mercy," she said, looking disgusted. "Are you fighting in God's house?"

Someone in the back of the small crowd yelled, "A shame before God, that's what it is."

Someone else mumbled, "Good Lord, they're gonna have this all on Media TakeOut-dot-com."

Rachel wanted to lunge at Mary again, but the sight of her children standing there, tears running down their cheeks, stopped her.

She looked around at the small crowd staring in horror. She closed her eyes, silently cursing what she had just done. This was exactly what Mary wanted.

"Come on, children, let's go," Rachel said, grabbing Jordan and Nia's hands and making her way toward the back of the church.

She ignored Twyla calling after her and had just reached the back door when Lester walked in.

"Hey, sweetheart. Sorry I'm late, I had—" He stopped midsentence when he noticed the disheveled look on her face and the terrified expressions on the children's faces. "What's going on?"

"Lester, I can't talk to you right now." Rachel started to walk around him and out the door.

Lester grabbed her arm to stop her. "Rachel, talk to me. What's the matter?"

She couldn't open her mouth to speak and instead covered her face as she burst into tears. Lester looked at the kids. "What is going on?" he repeated.

Nia wrapped her arms around her mother's leg and sobbed with her. Jordan finally spoke up. "Mommy and that other fat lady had a fight."

"What other fat lady?" Lester asked.

"That lady who's having a baby, too. The white lady," Jordan said.

Lester slowly looked up at Rachel. "Please tell me he's not saying what I think he's saying?"

"Lester, I have to go," she cried.

"Rachel, you're in no condition to drive."

"I need to get out of this building," she pleaded. She had worked so hard to leave this drama-filled, crazy life behind, and she was so disappointed that she'd let Mary push her buttons and make her revert to her old ways.

Before Lester could reply, Twyla, Deacon Baker and two other deacons came up to him. "Pastor Adams, there you are," Deacon Baker said. He looked at Rachel sympathetically, but then his expression hardened as he turned back to Lester.

"Pastor," he continued, "I understand that everybody makes mistakes, but this is unacceptable. I know you are the head of this church, but you have to get this situation under control."

"You sure do," Sister Hicks said, her heels clicking as she approached them. "Our First Lady is out there acting a common fool."

"I am right here, Sister Hicks," Rachel said, trying to dry her eyes.

"I know you are!" she snapped. "I see you. And you know me, what I have to say, I say to your face." She wagged her finger at Rachel. "What just happened now, that is a shame, a sin and a shame! Now, I'm sure any whuppin' you gave that woman she definitely had comin', but you can't go around beating up on women." She glared at Lester. "Even when you've been given just cause. You need to have some dignity and self-respect about all of this and know that God will work it all out!"

"Pastor, we stayed silent on this as long as we could, but this is absolutely unacceptable," added another deacon, Lionel Evans. "I've been knowing you and Rachel since before you came into this world. Rev. Jackson is gonna have a stroke when he hears about this."

Rachel shook her head, starting to feel exasperated. She knew she had overstepped the boundaries, but how much could any one woman be expected to take?

"You know what?" Rachel said, trying to compose herself. "I totally understand and I agree with you all." Everyone looked on in shock. She was sure no one expected her to agree with them, since she always had been the combative type. But she was tired. She was tired of being tortured by this woman. She was tired of having to take the high road, and she was through.

"You don't have to worry about any more problems with me and Mary here at Zion Hill," Rachel said.

Lester looked at her like he wasn't quite understanding what she was saying.

Rachel turned to her son. "Jordan, take your sister to the car. I'll be there in a minute." Jordan apprehensively grabbed Nia's hand and led her outside. As soon as the door closed, Rachel spun around and glared at her husband. "Let me break it down for you, Rev. Adams. Since you can't—or won't—ask that woman to leave this church, I will leave."

"Rachel, don't be ridiculous. You can't leave," Lester said.

She clutched her hands in front of her chest. "I'm not being ridiculous. Do you realize that I just jeopardized my future child by fighting with your former mistress?" She didn't care that the deacons, Sister Hicks, and a few other church members were staring. "I had a *fistfight* in church, in front of my children, while I'm eight months pregnant, with *another pregnant woman*! This is too much. And it's not getting any better. Do you understand me? If I am forced to attend church with that woman, I can't make any promises that I will keep on taking the high road. So, since it seems you can't get her under control and you won't put her out of the church, then I have to go."

Having laid down her ultimatum, Rachel stormed out the door and made her way to her car. She didn't know if Lester believed her or not, but she could definitely show him better than she could tell him. As long as Mary was a member of that church, she would never set foot in there again.

Chapter 12

Jonathan had his own dramas to deal with, so he wasn't in the right frame of mind to console his frustrated brother-in-law. But judging from the weary expression on Lester's face, Jonathan knew he had to do whatever he could to help out. Lester had come straight over from church and filled them in on what had happened.

"So what do you think I should do?" he said. "I mean, I know asking Mary to leave is just going to make her even madder and create more drama. And technically, because the church isn't regulated by a higher authority, I can't put her out."

Jonathan looked over at David, who was lying across his sofa. David had long ago tuned Lester out and was now trying to take a nap.

"Lester, I think you need to handle it. I know my sister, and I'm telling you, there is only so much more she's going to take," Jonathan said. "I'm surprised she hasn't tried to jump on Mary before this. It has to be because she's pregnant, but you'd better believe, if Rachel said she's not coming back to that church, she's not coming back. Come on, you've been married to her for seven years, you know this."

Lester released a long groan. "I know, but it's not that simple. I don't want to put Rachel through any more heartache than I already have. I know that what I did was wrong. I prayed for forgiveness, and thankfully, Rachel forgave me and took me back."

"Then making her happy should be your number-one priority."

"But what will the people at the church say about me running Mary off, especially if she causes a scene? I was just hoping she would go away on her own."

David shifted on the couch, blew a frustrated breath and finally sat up. "Look, I was going to stay out of this, considering the girl tried to play me as well. But you sound just like my daddy, putting that church first. And look where it got him." David was referring to the fact that the board at Zion Hill had tried to vote Simon out as pastor because he couldn't "get his kids under control." Simon had put that church first all of his life and, when he'd needed them most, they'd turned their back on him.

"You need to think about what's important," David said, swinging his feet onto the floor. "Now, I know Mary's crazy.

If she will go to the lengths of dating me to get to my sister, she's got some real serious issues. But if you keep going the way you've been going, the problem is only going to get worse. How would you feel if Rachel really hurt that girl and had to go to jail or something?"

Lester's eyes widened in horror.

"I don't think Rachel will do anything that extreme," Jonathan interjected.

"Please, we are talking about Rachel here," David said, lying back down on the sofa. "You believe that if you want to, but I'm telling you, my sister is on the edge. And if you don't get Mary under control, you're going to push her right over." David turned his back to them, indicating he'd said all he had to say.

Lester looked at Jonathan. "So, what do I do?"

"Have you tried talking to Mary?"

Lester nodded. "Plenty of times. She just won't leave us alone."

"No, I mean, *really* talking to her? Show her you mean business," Jonathan said.

"You know you soft, boy," David called up from the couch. "You better let her know you ain't playing."

"David's right," Jonathan added. "You have to tell her that she can try all she wants, but you're not leaving your wife. And ask her nicely to leave the church."

"Hah!" David laughed, his back still to them. "That girl don't know nothing about being nice."

"Ignore my brother," Jonathan continued. "I think that's what you should do."

Lester contemplated what Jonathan was saying. "Do you think David's right?" he asked. "Am I really soft?"

"I told you, don't listen to David. You're not like that at all. Didn't you put your foot down when Deacon Jacobs wanted to strong-arm the board into agreeing on mandatory tithing?"

Lester slowly nodded. "I did. And I stood up to Lori Angleton's abusive husband," he said, as if he was just remembering.

"Right, so if you could get some backbone in those situations, surely you can get Mary under control."

"Okay, maybe you're right." Lester began pulling out his cell phone. "I don't know why I'm letting this woman get to me. I'll convince her to leave on her own. I'll call her now and explain how I'm not going to stand for her games."

"No." Jonathan snapped Lester's cell phone shut. "Go talk to her face-to-face."

"You think I should go over there?" Lester asked in amazement.

"If you want to be eaten alive," David chimed in.

Jonathan cut his eyes at his brother's back. "Don't listen to him. Yes, you should go over there. You need to look her in the eye and tell her it's over. Tell her it's time to move on. Remind her that if the baby is yours—"

Lester buried his head in his hands.

"If the baby is yours," Jonathan continued, "you're going to take care of your child. But regardless, she has to leave Zion Hill."

"Don't do it," David warned. "You'd be better off hiring somebody to kill her."

"My brother is kidding. Murder is not an option. Just go talk to her in person," Jonathan reiterated. "Over the phone, she's not going to take you seriously."

An idea hit Lester. "And I'll tell her that if she comes near Rachel again, I'll get a restraining order against her. Come to think of it, maybe that's what I need anyway, you know, to keep her away from the church."

"Like a piece of paper is gonna stop her," David mumbled.

Lester ignored him as his resolve strengthened. "That's what I'll do. That's how I will bring this drama to an end."

"That's what I'm talking about," Jonathan said as he stood to walk Lester to the door. "Put an end to all of this."

Lester nodded emphatically as relief seemed to pour off his body.

Jonathan noticed David shaking his head, but he didn't say anything. Lester was displaying a confidence they hadn't seen in a while. And Lord knows, he was going to need it if he was truly going to get that psycho Mary under control.

Chapter 13

Rachel took a deep breath before walking into the office. She had thought long and hard about what she was about to do, and while she didn't want to play around with God, she definitely had to show these folks she meant business.

"Hi, may I help you?" the perky secretary asked. She was seated behind a large oak desk, a mountain of paperwork in front of her.

"Yes, I'm here to see Pastor Ellis."

The woman smiled. "Do you have an appointment?"

"I don't. I was just hoping to talk with the pastor."

"Your name, please, and I'll see if he's available."

"It's umm, Rachel, Rachel Jackson Adams."

The woman's eyes widened in recognition. "From Zion—"

"Yes," Rachel said, cutting her off.

"What shall I say you'd like to meet with him about?" the woman asked, all ears now. "Pastor is very particular and likes for me to get as many details as possible."

Rachel was about to reply with a sarcastic remark when an idea dawned on her. This couldn't have worked out better if she had planned it. Pastor Ellis would never put her business in the street, but this woman looked like she was dying for some good gossip.

"Yes," Rachel said, feigning a smile. "I'm looking to move my membership."

"Okay," the woman said, pretending to write on her note-pad. "So, I can tell Pastor you *and* your husband are looking to join us at Lily Grove?"

"No, my husband will stay at Zion Hill. It's just me leaving," Rachel said, giving the woman what she wanted. She was tired of people feeling sorry for her, and maybe if they saw she was leaving Zion Hill, they'd know she wasn't just going to sit back and let her husband's former mistress taunt her.

The woman was struggling to contain her excitement. "Okay, wait right here," she said, standing up. "I'll go check with Pastor Ellis."

She disappeared for a few minutes, then returned with a big grin. "Pastor can see you right now." She motioned toward the door.

Rachel nodded. She knew that as soon as she walked into the office, that woman would be on the phone spreading the news that there was trouble in paradise for Rev. Adams and his wife. Rachel didn't care. How could she be embarrassed any more than she already had been?

"Well, Sister Adams, it's mighty lovely to see you here today." Pastor Terrance Ellis stood to greet her as she walked in. He was a handsome man, six feet tall with strong features, smooth, coffee-brown skin and cheekbones that could cut glass.

"Hi, Rev. Ellis, thank you for seeing me without an appointment."

"No, when my secretary said it was you, I knew this had to be pretty important." He motioned toward the chair in front of his desk.

"It is," Rachel said, taking a seat. When she was settled in, she cleared her throat. "I imagine you've heard about the drama over at Zion Hill."

He sat down and looked at her with compassion. "I've heard some rumblings, but you know I don't dwell in gossip."

"Well," Rachel began, "you know most gossip is rooted in truth."

"I imagine that to be true, but there's no need for individuals to allow it to flourish." He paused, waiting for her to say something. When she didn't, he went on. "My secretary said you wanted to talk about moving your membership."

Rachel's eyes drifted to her lap. "Yes, I need to get out of that church."

"And what does Pastor Adams have to say about that?"

"Who cares what he has to say?" she said sullenly. "What he wants doesn't matter anymore."

"In the eyes of God it does."

Rachel rolled her eyes, then caught herself. "Look, it's either move my membership or stop coming to church altogether. And since I've come a long way in my journey, I'd like to keep coming to church."

Rev. Ellis gave her that sincere look again. "Haven't you been in Zion Hill literally all your life?"

"And nothing has gotten any better," she informed him.

He sighed, scratching his forehead a few times. "Okay, I understand your feelings, but let's backtrack a bit. Let's talk about what's really bothering you."

"I-I told you. I want to move my membership," Rachel stammered.

"Have you talked to someone about how you're feeling? The reason behind your wanting to move."

Rachel knew where he was going with this conversation, but she hadn't come here to indulge in a counseling session.

"Rachel," he said, getting up and moving close to her, "I know you may feel betrayed by Lester." He took her hand. "I understand your anger at him, and there is only one way for you to get over that anger. To move past the pain." His left hand went to her thigh.

Rachel was taken aback. Was Pastor Ellis coming on to her? Did she still have it going on—at eight months pregnant? She knew he was married—his search for a wife had made news all over town. But maybe he was like these other no-good preachers, including her own husband. Maybe he liked having a little extra on the side. Rachel thought about how she should react. Maybe that's what she needed to get over Lester's affair—an affair of her own. Technically, she'd never cheated on Lester. She'd tried to do it once with Bobby, but she'd backed out at the last minute. But maybe that had been because she and Bobby had history. Maybe she needed someone she had no connection to. Maybe she needed the fine man feeling her leg.

"So you think it's possible to get over this?" she said slowly.

"I know it is," he said with a smile. He was so sexy and his eyes were inviting. She felt a small tingle inside. "And I want to help you do it," Pastor Ellis continued.

She looked at him in alarm, then quickly shook away any doubt. If she thought about why she shouldn't too long, she'd talk herself out of it. And if her being pregnant didn't bother him, it wouldn't bother her.

"Okay," she finally said.

"How about we start right now?" he said, walking over to lock the door. "I'm locking the door to give us some privacy, because I don't want you to have any reservations."

Rachel fought off the butterflies that sprang up inside her stomach. Was he actually going to try and get it on with her in his office, with his secretary just outside the door? Maybe that added to the excitement.

"Okay," she replied as she stood and smoothed her dress down. If this man couldn't make her feel better, no one could.

He walked back over and stood in front of her. "I want you to forget all your troubles. Just let yourself go. Close your eyes," he ordered.

She closed her eyes and inhaled as he took both her hands and moved in closer. Her heart was racing and she readied herself for his kiss. It had been a long time since another man's lips had touched hers. Would this really make her feel better? Would this help her get over her pain? *Stop trying to talk yourself out of it,* she told herself.

"Heavenly Father, I come to you in prayer today for Your child . . . ," Rev. Ellis began.

Rachel's eyes shot open. Rev. Ellis was standing in front of her, gripping her hands, his eyes closed, deep in prayer.

". . . we humbly ask that you remove this anger . . ."

Rachel quickly closed her eyes. Was this how preachers started their seductions?

". . . come on, Rachel, don't be ashamed. He knows your pain. Tell Him how you feel, get it out," Rev. Ellis urged as he continued praying.

Rachel managed to mutter a few "Thank you, Jesus's." He really was praying. She'd read the situation all wrong. As he droned on, all she wanted was to get out of that office. She couldn't believe this. She was so embarrassed. What if she had leaned in to kiss him? What kind of woman was she that she was ready to make out with a married pastor in his church office—and at eight months pregnant?

Rachel didn't hear the rest of his prayer, she was trying so hard not to bust out of her skin in shame.

". . . in Jesus's name. Amen," Rev. Ellis wrapped up.

Rachel opened her eyes to the smiling minister. "Now, if prayer can't remove that pain and bitterness, I don't know what can."

Rachel was too stunned to open her mouth.

"What's the matter?" he asked as he looked at her strangely.

"N-nothing." She grabbed her purse out of the other seat. "Thank you for that prayer." She scurried toward the door.

He seemed mildly put off by her retreat. "I know it was a little intense, but I felt some spiritual warfare going on and I wanted us to give it our all."

Rachel simply nodded as she reached for the doorknob. He reached out and placed his hand on her arm. His touch made her want to cry.

"You call or come see me anytime, okay?"

She nodded. That was about the last thing she was ever going to do.

"And do me one other favor. Hold off on moving that membership." He gently patted her belly. "My beautiful wife is pregnant, so I know how you women can be when your hormones are running rampant. You can make some rash decisions."

If only you knew, Rachel thought. She didn't want to engage in any more conversation. Right about now, all she wanted was to get out of that office before he somehow figured out what she had really been thinking.

"Thank you, Rev. Ellis, so much," she said before racing out of his office as fast as she could.

Chapter 14

Mary wasn't surprised to see Lester on her doorstep. She'd figured the incident at church would send him running to see her. That was what she'd been hoping for. Maybe now he could see what a deranged lunatic his wife was. Mary just needed to get Lester alone, talk to him and remind him of how things had been back when Rachel had been neglecting him and she'd been there to pick up the pieces and comfort him. She needed to remind Lester that she knew how a real man should be treated. She'd been hoping to do that after church yesterday, but he hadn't stuck around after the service.

"Hey, baby," Mary said, throwing her arms around Lester's neck.

Lester stiffly removed her arms, then pushed his way past her and into her apartment. He stopped in the middle of her living room and turned to face her. He had a stern, serious look that she'd never seen before. "Mary, let me be very clear that this is not a social call," Lester said with conviction. "Now look, I try my best not to tell someone where they can and cannot worship the Lord, but you do not need to come back to Zion Hill."

She closed her front door and wobbled over to him. She was a little sore and didn't know if it was because of the fight or the fact that the doctor she'd seen this morning had told her that the baby had dropped. "You have got to be kidding me," she said. "You can't keep me out of church."

"Unfortunately, we can do anything we want. And if we need to get a restraining order against you, then we'll do that."

"A restraining order against me?" she asked incredulously. "Are you for real? It's that psycho wife of yours that needs a restraining order! She attacked me. I should press charges against her."

"All I know is that if you come anywhere near me, the church, or my wife, you will regret it."

Mary would've been furious if the situation hadn't been so comical. She broke out in a huge smile. "Look at you, trying to be macho." She ran her finger across his chest. "I actually like this hardness about you."

He shrank away from her hand. "I came here in person because I don't want to embarrass you in church by having you served or anything like that. Plus, I was hoping to just plead with you as a reasonable adult."

Mary crossed her arms over her chest, resting them on her protruding belly.

"I just want the drama to stop, and the best way for that to happen is for you to find a new church home," he continued.

"But if you ask the board to agree to a restraining order, won't that make things a little tense when I become First Lady?" she calmly replied.

"Mary, you are delusional," he exclaimed. "You will never be First Lady, at least not my First Lady."

She took a moment to process that statement, then said, "Can I get you something to drink? Some white zinfandel, perhaps? And don't try to act like you don't drink." She smiled coyly. "Because I remember the night our baby was conceived." She rubbed her stomach. "We had quite a bit of zinfandel. Well, you only had three glasses." She playfully poked him in the stomach. "Lightweight."

He recoiled from her. "Are you listening to anything that I'm saying to you?"

She shrugged nonchalantly, then walked into the kitchen. "I hear you, Lester, and all I'm saying is, can we have one last drink before you kick me out of your life?"

He rubbed his head in exasperation. "Mary—"

"It's not going to kill you to have one drink." She smiled seductively. "You can watch me so you can be sure that I don't try to drug you or anything."

"I don't want anything to drink," he said sternly.

"Well, I hope you don't mind if I get something. And before you get your feathers in a ruffle, my doctor said one glass of wine will not hurt me. Besides, you're over here delivering this devastating news, so I think that I'm entitled to a glass of wine."

Lester sighed heavily and followed her into the kitchen. "Mary, I'm not trying to make things hard on you."

She spun back toward him. "Well, you are." She hadn't meant to get upset, but her emotions had a habit of jumping from one extreme to the other these days. "I love you, Lester, and you can say what you want, but I know you love me, too. Or you at least used to love me."

"Let's not play games, Mary," Lester replied with an edge. "We both know that your trying to get with me was all a big sham from the start. And even though I'm a man of God, my brief affair with you was the product of nothing but loneliness and lust."

She wiped the tear that had begun trickling down her cheek. "Yes, it started out that way, but you know that what we had was real." She stepped closer to him. She wanted him to smell her, feel her. Maybe that would make him remember what they had. "Look into my soul and tell me that it wasn't real."

Pity filled his eyes. "Yes, I cared for you, but I was vulnerable and in a really bad place. Still, that's no excuse. I handled the problems in my marriage the wrong way. It was a mistake that I will regret the rest of my life."

She rubbed her stomach again. "So, you really believe our baby is a mis—" Mary jumped as the baby planted a firm kick in the side of her stomach.

"Wh-what's wrong?" He was eyeing her skeptically, like he wasn't sure whether she was faking. But that had been a real kick. It was like the baby was on her side. A huge smile crossed

Mary's face as she lifted her blouse to reveal her bare stomach. "He's getting worked up."

Lester stared at her stomach, wide-eyed. "It . . . it's moving."

"He does that a lot," Mary said, watching her stomach move as her baby tried to turn over. Seizing the moment, she stepped toward him. "If you're going to get a restraining order against me and not allow me anywhere near you, at least feel your son one time."

When Lester didn't move, she took his hand and gently placed it on her stomach. He seemed mesmerized as her stomach moved up and down. Mary's heart fluttered when he didn't pull his hand away. She couldn't contain herself. She moved in and quickly planted a kiss on his full lips. She kissed him hard and long and she couldn't be sure, but it almost felt like he was kissing her back. But then he forcefully grabbed her and pushed her away. "What are you doing?" he hissed.

"What comes naturally," she said, reaching up to kiss him again.

Lester looked at her in disgust, then turned and stomped out of the kitchen. "It was a mistake coming over here."

She took off after him, grabbing him just as he entered the living room. "I felt you kiss me back. You want me!" she exclaimed. "You want us."

Lester spun toward her and growled, "Get this through your thick skull. It is over! I don't want you," he said, grabbing her forearms tightly.

She bruised easily and knew the force would leave marks,

93

but she didn't care. She had to get through to him. "You don't know what you want," she said, trying to kiss him again.

"Get off me!" he said, pushing her firmly away.

She was leaning forward so hard that the force caused her to lose her footing. She stumbled backward, then was tripped by the glass coffee table. As she toppled onto it, the glass shattered into a million little pieces. Mary let out a piercing scream.

"Mary!" Lester called out.

She immediately felt a sharp pain in the side of her stomach and looked down to see blood gushing out.

"Oh, my God!" she wailed, her hand instinctively moving to the bleeding area. "My baby . . ." Then she noticed a piece of glass that had lodged in her side, and she became panic-stricken. "Ohmigod!" Just the thought of losing her baby made her start hyperventilating.

"I'm sorry, God," she cried. "Please, don't take my baby."

Lester dropped to the floor next to her. "Mary, calm down! I'm calling for help," he said, fumbling to get his cell phone out of his jacket pocket.

Mary was hysterical as Lester called 9-1-1. She couldn't make out what he was saying, nor could she even tell how much time had passed, but the next thing she knew, Lester had taken off his shirt and was using it to apply pressure to stop the bleeding.

Mary felt herself blacking out. She didn't know if it was because of the shock or the blood she'd lost. All she knew was that right before darkness took over, she found herself saying a prayer for God to save her child.

Chapter 15

Lester looked like he had never been so relieved in his life.

"Hey, how are you?" he asked, easing into Mary's hospital room.

"Much better," she said. She was nursing her baby, who was wrapped tightly in a light blue blanket. The past five hours had been the most frightening of her life. The glass had pierced her amniotic sac and they'd had to induce labor. But everything had turned out fine. A healthy Lester Adams Jr. had come into this world weighing six pounds, ten ounces. "I'm just glad he's all right." She gently stroked his cheek.

"You and me both," Lester said, peering over at the infant.

"Do you want to hold him?" Mary offered.

Lester was touched by the sight of the baby boy, then said, "I'd better not."

Mary smiled. "Come on. It's not going to kill you to hold him." For once, she wasn't playing games. She genuinely wanted Lester to feel what she felt right now. Pure unadulterated love for their son. She held the baby out toward him.

Lester hesitated before extending his arms and taking the baby from her.

"He has your eyes and your nose," Mary said.

Lester squinted like he was studying the baby. "He's pale."

"He's biracial, silly," Mary replied. "Babies are naturally light anyway."

Lester was about to respond when the hospital room door opened and a petite West Indies nurse walked in. A sly grin crossed her face when she noticed Lester. "Well hello, there," she said with a heavy accent.

"Hello," Lester said uneasily.

The nurse walked over to Mary and picked up her chart. "How are the mother and baby?"

"We're doing fine," Mary said. "Especially now," she added, looking at Lester.

The nurse looked like she was fighting back a smile as she watched Lester holding the baby.

"Well, it's time for little Lester to go get some tests," she said as she gently took the baby. "I will bring your baby right back."

As soon as she left the room, Lester spun toward Mary. "You named him Lester?"

"Yes, I did. I happen to like that name."

Lester rubbed his forehead, irritated all over again. "That wasn't a good idea," he mumbled.

"I don't know why not," Mary said. She turned up her lips when he didn't answer. "Oh, I know why. You want a DNA test first." She leaned back in the bed. "Well, that's how confident I am. And there's no sense in changing his name after the DNA test, especially when I know what the results will say."

Lester let out a long, exasperated sigh. "You know what? I need to get going. I need to get home."

"So you're just going to leave?"

He shot her a look that said what else did she expect? "Bye, Mary. I'll be in touch."

"Lester, wait. Before you go . . ." She leaned over and pulled a piece of paper off the nightstand. "I need you to sign this Acknowledgment of Paternity." She'd made it a point to ask for the document right after the delivery.

"You need me to do what?" he asked.

She waved the paper at him. "I need you to sign this form. I don't want my child to leave this hospital a bastard child."

He wasn't moving one inch toward her. "I'm sorry, Mary, but I'm not going to be able to do that. At least not until the DNA results come back," he said matter-of-factly.

Mary studied his face. He was serious. Dead serious. That left her with only one other choice, one she'd hoped she wouldn't have to use. She reached over and pulled the telephone to her lap.

"What are you doing?" Lester asked.

She nestled the phone between her ear and shoulder and began punching in numbers. "Calling the police."

Lester raced over to her bedside and snatched the phone away. "Calling the police for what?"

She shrugged, then held out her hand for the phone. "Attempted murder, assault, I don't know."

He pulled the phone out of her reach. "What? You've got to be kidding me."

"No, I'm not." She pushed up the sleeve on her hospital gown to show him the large bruises on both of her arms. "These are from when you grabbed me earlier." She moved the hospital gown to the side to reveal the fresh stitches in the side of her stomach where the glass had cut her. "This is from where you threw me down onto a coffee table and almost killed me and my child. And this"—she pointed to an older bruise around her neck that Lester hadn't noticed before—"well, it's a long story, but I have no problem saying you did this, too."

His mouth was hanging open. "Mary, you know I didn't intentionally hurt you. And I can't believe you would lie."

Tears started to fill her eyes. "I don't know anything," she calmly began, "except that you were so desperate for me not to have this child and cause any more problems in your life that you came over to my house in a rage and demanded that I move away. And when I refused . . ." Mary stopped and fake coughed. "When I refused . . . you just lost it." She summoned up a pitiful look on her face. "Your Honor, all I wanted was to have my baby and have Rev. Adams be a part of his life," she said in a slow, Southern drawl. "I mean he's a minister and I

98

just went to him for counseling. I wasn't planning to have sex with him because he's married. But I was vulnerable. And he took advantage of that . . . and I just never in a million years would've thought he could have such rage. My precious baby is just lucky to be alive." She stopped and gave him a wry smile. "Do you think that's convincing enough?" He didn't have to answer. She knew it was. And judging from the horrified expression on Lester's face, he knew it was convincing, too.

"Nobody is going to believe you," he half-whispered. Even as the words left his mouth, he knew that they would. And even if they didn't, the scandal would destroy him—and his marriage.

"Oh, I'm sure they'll believe me. I can be pretty convincing, not to mention all the drama that it will cause you. You know, I can see the headline on CNN now—esteemed pastor attacks mistress. You know the media doesn't care about the truth, they just want a sensational story. And I'm sure Rachel will be like all those politicians' wives on the news who stand by their man while they deal with their cheating coming to light."

The mention of Rachel made his eyes grow wide. "I can't believe you would do that," Lester muttered in disbelief.

"I can't believe you would dare deny my child," she shot back.

Lester sighed in defeat. "What do you want, Mary? What do you want from me?"

"I want you to acknowledge your child," she said bluntly.

"I'll do that. I just want a DNA test, that's all."

"I told you I would have a DNA test when I'm ready to

have one. But you weren't asking for a DNA test when you laid down with me. I don't want my child to be denied."

Lester lowered his head as his shoulders deflated.

"Just give him a name," she urged. "Sign the paper."

"I can't acknowledge paternity yet."

"Sign the paper, or the cops will be waiting for you by the time you get downstairs."

Lester looked at her with pure hate. She had hoped to never play this card, but he'd left her with no choice. It had always been her final card—and the fact that he'd left bruises on her when he'd grabbed her was just icing on the cake. Bernice had told Mary that she might not even be entitled to child support until she could prove the baby was his. Sure, a DNA test would do that, but so would this Acknowledgment of Paternity. And she couldn't take any chances.

"Lester?" She shook the paper at him. "If the baby isn't yours, you can have the acknowledgment rescinded later."

Lester snatched the paper from her. "I can't believe you're doing this."

"Believe it," she said.

He glared at her one last time before scrawling his signature on the bottom of the paper. She smiled in triumph as she took the paper from him. "That's all I wanted, for my child to have a father." She folded the paper up. "Now you can go back home to your wife and your nice peaceful existence, and I will leave you alone."

Lester looked at her skeptically.

Say Amen, Again

"Go, Lester. I'm sure you need to get home to your wife. You've been gone a long time."

He looked like he was unsure of what to do. Finally, he said, "Fine. We will be in touch about a DNA test."

Mary nodded dutifully. When she heard her door slam, she couldn't help but smile. "I wouldn't wait on that DNA test, Rev. Adams." She pulled the Acknowledgment of Paternity close to her chest. This was all the test she needed, whether Lester liked it or not.

Chapter 16

Jonathan wished that he had never opened his front door. By no means did he want to be disrespectful, but the sight of his aunt Minnie and the four equally obtrusive-looking women standing behind her told him this was not going to be a pleasant visit.

"Aunt Minnie, how are you?" Jonathan asked, feigning a smile.

"Blessed and highly favored," she said, her eyes roaming up and down his body. He hadn't seen his aunt in years. She'd broken her hip and missed his mom's funeral, and there had been no other family gatherings for them to cross paths since then. The way she was scouring him, though, disgust across her face, told him that she knew all about his being gay.

"What brings you, and um, your friends by?" Jonathan said

when it became obvious that the women weren't going to introduce themselves.

Minnie folded her arms across her chest. With the exception of the graying hair, she looked exactly the same as she always had. "We missed you at dinner."

"Yeah, I wasn't able to make it. I had something come up," Jonathan said nervously. When he was a child, his aunt had been the mean relative that everyone had run from. Luckily, she didn't visit often, nor did they go to her home in Alabama, so their contact was minimal.

"Pitiful that you can't make time for family."

"Well, what can I help you with?" Jonathan shifted uncomfortably but didn't move to invite them in. "I was about to head out."

"Then we got here just in time," she said, bogarting her way past Jonathan.

"Sisters, take your position," she ordered. The four women all went to separate corners of Jonathan's living room.

Jonathan took a deep breath and readied for the battle he knew he was about to endure. "Can somebody please tell me what's going on?"

"These are some prayer warriors I've enlisted," she said, pleased with herself. "When you're on God's team, no matter where you go, you can find someone to do battle with. They're here to help me win this war."

"I'm sorry, come again?" Jonathan said.

"These are my prayer warriors," she said louder, as if he

hadn't actually heard her the first time. "We are interceding on your behalf."

"I'm sorry, I didn't know my behalf needed interceding," Jonathan replied.

"It does," one of the women said, shooting him an annoyed look. She was about sixty-five, her hair snow white and curled tightly. She wore a paisley dress and a wooden crucifix around her neck.

Jonathan decided not to even dignify the woman with a response. "Aunt Minnie, I really was just about to head out," he protested. "Maybe we can get together another time." He didn't want to be rude, but his aunt was the most judgmental person he knew—despite the fact that she claimed to be the biggest Christian—and he wasn't in the mood to deal with her and her weirdo pals.

"Jonathan, we're not going to take long. We just came to pray for you," Minnie said. "We'll start there. With prayer."

"Thank you, but I'm good."

"No, you ain't," one of the other women snapped. She walked over and nudged Minnie, who stepped forward and handed Jonathan two books.

"Here," Minnie said.

Jonathan took the books reluctantly. "What's this?" His mouth dropped open when he read the titles. "*You Don't Have to Be Gay* and *Homosexual No More*?" He pulled out a flyer advertising a meeting to "Pray the Gay Away." Jonathan looked at his aunt in amazement. "Are you for real?"

"God has laid it on our hearts to help you through this iniquity," Minnie declared.

"He can deliver you from your disease," the white-haired lady added.

Jonathan looked from one woman to another. "You're kidding, right?"

"We wouldn't joke about something of this magnitude," Minnie said.

"And it's not a joking matter! Hallelujah!" one of the women still in the corner shouted as she waved a Bible back and forth in the air.

Jonathan couldn't believe the nerve of these women. His aunt was bad enough. But these other women—whom he didn't even know—were definitely out of order.

"You know what? I think you all really need to leave," Jonathan demanded. Forget being nice. They were history.

"We'll go in a minute," Minnie said. "But let me ask you, don't you want to go to Heaven?"

He couldn't believe she was asking him this. He tortured himself all the time, but to have someone sit in judgment . . .

"I don't want this," he found himself saying. "Number one, shouldn't God be the only one judging me?"

"I—"

"Number two," he continued, cutting his aunt off. "Do you really think that I just woke up one day and decided, 'Oh, I want to be gay'? 'I want to disappoint my family.' 'I want to disappoint my father.' 'I want to be outcast from society.' Do you think I processed all of that and still said, 'Let me *decide* to be gay'?"

"It is a choice," she said with finality.

Jonathan let out a heavy sigh. He didn't even know why he was trying to reason with these so-called prayer warriors.

"Aunt Minnie, I'm going to ask you one more time, please leave my house."

She had the nerve to look like she had an attitude.

"Fine," she huffed, tucking her Bible under her arm. "If you want eternal damnation, then so be it."

Jonathan didn't respond as he held the door open for her and the other women to leave.

They defiantly marched past, each glaring at him as they exited. Jonathan had never been so relieved to see the back side of anyone. He had just closed the door when his telephone rang. He debated not answering it but figured it was Angela, his ex-wife, letting him know what time he could pick up Chase today to take him to Jordan's baseball game.

"Hello," he said into the phone.

"Hey, Jonathan," Angela replied. "Chase is all yours and ready to go. But he wanted me to tell you to make sure that you bring his blue Dallas Cowboys jersey. He's been having a fit for it and doesn't want to go to the game without it."

A small smile bloomed on his face. "How my son's gonna be a Cowboys fan is beyond me," he said. "Doesn't he know that Texans are the team?"

"Maybe if they win this season, he'll get behind them." She laughed. "In the meantime, though, this little boy is a Cowboys fan all the way."

It felt so good to hear Angela laugh. For years she had

hated him with every ounce of her being and right-fully so.

"Good point." Jonathan loudly exhaled, the smile leaving his voice. "Okay, I'll make sure it's there."

Angela responded to the shift in his tone. "What's wrong with you? You sound a little down."

"Oh, I just had an unwelcome visit from one of my relatives," he said, massaging his temples.

"Oh, really? Who?"

"My aunt Minnie. You know, my dad's sister, the religious nut from Alabama."

"Oh yeah," Angela said. "I remember meeting her at your high school graduation. She just stopped by to say hello?"

"Unfortunately, she's staying with my dad awhile and she came to see me to pray for my soul. She started talking to me about—" Jonathan stopped himself. While Angela had become cordial to him, his sexuality was a conversation they never broached. He never brought up the painful subject and neither did she.

"Let's just say she wants to pray for my soul," Jon said.

"Oh," Angela replied, knowing where he was going with that. "Well, I'm glad you got rid of her. Look, I have to run, but Chase will be at my mom's house."

"Aww, man, your mother's?" Jonathan said. While Angela had gotten over her hatred, her parents had not.

"I'm so sorry to do this to you, but we don't have much choice. Steve got the time wrong on our flight out, and so my mom is just going to take him on to her house. She's in the same place in Lake Olympia. Just ignore her and everything will be fine."

Jonathan sighed heavily. He somehow doubted that. "All right. Have a safe trip." They said their good-byes and Jon went back to straightening up his living room. He glanced at the books his aunt had given him, shook his head, then walked over and dumped them in the kitchen trash can. The flyer drifted free and fell at his feet. The words glared at him. "Pray the Gay Away." The prospect was eerie, like something out of the movies. It sounded crazy, but the more Jonathan thought about the idea, the more he began to wonder: could his aunt Minnie have a point? Could you really pray the gay away? If that's all it took, Jonathan was definitely willing to try. He picked the flyer up, folded it, and tucked it in his pocket.

Chapter 17

The words echoed in Rachel's head. *I ain't one to gossip, so you ain't heard this from me . . .*

As Carmen Washington uttered those words, Rachel knew she was in for some juicy gossip. She just had no idea the gossip would involve her own husband.

Carmen acted like it pained her to share the phone call that she'd just gotten from her sister, a nurse at Hermann Hospital.

"I mean, I don't have any idea what Rev. Adams must've been thinking going into that hospital with that woman."

The blow struck Rachel like a hammer. She almost forgot that Carmen was still on the phone.

"Sister Adams, I am so sorry to be bringing you this sad, sad news. I prayed over it and the Lord said, 'Carmen, you've got to tell her.' So I did." She swallowed hard. "If there's anything I can do, you just let me know."

Rachel couldn't believe this woman. Yeah, she knew Carmen from around church, but not to the point where the woman should feel "led" to call her about something so personal.

"No, I'm okay," Rachel said. She thought about lying and saying she knew Lester had gone there, but she couldn't get the words to form. The idea was absolutely appalling.

"Is there somebody I can call for you?" Carmen asked.

Other than the list of people you're going to call and spread the gossip to as soon as you hang up the phone with me? Rachel wanted to ask. Instead she said, "No, I'll be fine. Thanks for calling."

"As soon as my sister called and told me that Rev. Adams was up in that room with that woman, I just knew I had to call my First Lady," Carmen continued.

Rachel cut her off before she could say anything else. "Okay, I appreciate that. Thank you, but I really need to go."

"Okay, First Lady. I'm going to keep you in my prayers."

"Thank you very much," Rachel replied. With trembling fingers she placed the phone back on its cradle. *I will not go into a frenzy. I will not go into a frenzy.* Rachel closed her eyes and kept repeating that to herself. But the more she said it, the more she got worked up. She felt her baby move, so she began to rub her stomach, trying to calm down herself and her baby. She let out a deep breath when her blood pressure lost some steam, then reached for the phone again. She punched in Lester's number. When he didn't answer, she found herself repeating the calming mantra over and over.

Rachel didn't realize how long her thoughts had been trapped in this tight ring when she heard someone banging on the front door. She pulled herself up off the sofa and shuffled over to the door. David was standing there looking confused.

"What's going on?" he asked, perplexed. "I've been out here for almost fifteen minutes. I saw you inside and couldn't understand why you weren't answering the door. I was just about to break the door down."

"I'm sorry," Rachel said, leaving the door open for him to follow her in. "I just have a lot on my mind."

"Where's DJ?" David asked.

Rachel had almost forgotten her nephew was there. "He's upstairs asleep in the room with Nia."

He peered closely at her. "What has you looking like you're going crazy?"

Rachel clenched her fists. "It's that tramp you called a girlfriend."

He rolled his eyes. "Look, I apologized about that. I had no idea."

"Maybe if you went to church sometime, you would have known."

"Okay," he said, holding up his hands in defense, "don't bite my head off."

Rachel relented and inhaled deeply. "I'm sorry. I'm not upset with you. I know you didn't know." She began pacing back and forth. "I'm just furious right now. This woman is at the hospital, and some kind of way she's gotten Lester to come be with her while she had her baby."

"What? Why is he in the hospital?"

"That's the million-dollar question."

"Well, he said he was . . ." David let his words trail off.

"He said what?" Rachel snapped.

David blinked nervously. "Umm, I was just saying, why did he tell you he went to the hospital?"

"I haven't talked to him."

"Maybe you should talk to him before you get worked up in a tizzy."

She shook her head tightly. "Oh, it's too late for that."

"Rach, all I'm saying is, hear the man out. You don't know what happened. You don't know why he ended up at the hospital with her. Just give him a chance to explain before you start going off."

She shot David a look like he had to know better than that. No amount of explaining could justify Lester being at the hospital with that woman as she delivered her baby.

David rolled his eyes like he knew there would be no getting through to his little sister. "You know what? Let me get my child and get out of here before the drama jumps off."

"That probably would be wise," she said. "And take Nia with you. Jordan is over a friend's. The kids need to be gone because I promise you, when Lester gets home, it's not going to be pretty."

David hurried toward the stairs to retrieve his son and niece. "We'll all be long gone."

Chapter 18

Rachel watched through the window as her husband paced back and forth on the front porch. She knew he was working up the nerve to come inside. Probably trying to get his lie together.

She made her way downstairs, saying yet another quick prayer for the patience to not go off the minute he set foot in the door. She poured a cup of hot tea—chamomile, for her nerves—and sat down on the sofa.

That's where she was when Lester finally decided to come inside ten minutes later.

"Umm, hi, sweetie." He was startled to see her sitting so quietly on the sofa. That alone should have told him something was wrong. "Are you okay?" he asked when she didn't respond. She'd been in a funk since the fight at church, so the calm demeanor on her face made him clutch his hands uneasily. Rachel made a decision right then that before she lost it, she would give him a chance to admit the truth.

"Hey," she replied, mustering up a smile. He leaned over and tried to kiss her on her lips, but she deftly turned her head and let his lips meet her cheek. He stepped back and said, "How was your day?" He was studying her, no doubt trying to see if she knew anything.

"It was fine," she replied. "And yours?"

"Ummm, interesting," he stammered.

"Interesting? How so?" She flashed a fake smile again.

That seemed to make him relax some. "I just had a long day, that's all," he said, loosening his tie.

"Well, why don't you sit down and tell me all about it?"

He longingly looked toward the stairs. "Oh, well, I ah, wanted to get upstairs and see the kids before they went to sleep."

"They're not here. Nia went with David, and Jordan is still over his little friend's house."

"Oh." He hesitated. "Well, I probably should go upstairs anyway and work on my sermon for Sunday."

"No, no, come on, have a seat." She patted the sofa next to her. "I think we should talk. We haven't really talked since I left church."

Lester begrudgingly sat down.

"So what was interesting about your day?" Rachel asked as he slowly began removing his loose tie.

He looked terrified. "Well, I just had a bunch of stuff, ah, going on at church."

Rachel bit down on her bottom lip. "So, just church stuff, huh?"

Lester paused, his eyes darting everywhere. "Umm, yeah. But I'll talk to you about it in a minute. I really have a headache, and I want to run upstairs and get some aspirin."

He jumped into action, and Rachel watched as he walked to the stairway. She could not believe he was going to lie to her.

She followed him upstairs into their bedroom. He was still fumbling with the tie. He seemed to have lost all coordination. She walked over and started slowly helping him remove it. "So, have you had a chance to talk to Mary yet?" The only conversation they'd had the last few days was Lester telling her that he would ask Mary to leave Zion Hill and begging her to reconsider her decision to stay away.

His eyes dropped down to her hands on the tie, which she was supposed to have been loosening. "No . . . ," he slowly began.

"No?" she said, pulling the tie tighter.

He grabbed her arms to stop her. "I mean, yes. I . . . ummm, I can explain."

Rachel dropped her hands. She'd had enough. She stomped over to her walk-in closet. She reached in the back and pulled out her Louis Vuitton oversize suitcase.

"Rachel, what are you doing?"

"What does it look like, genius?" she said calmly.

"Where are you going?"

"Out. Away from your no-good, lying behind."

He stood in front of her with his mouth open.

She put her free hand on her hip. "What? You're speech-less now?" She dumped the suitcase at the foot of the bed. She stomped over to the drawer and began removing some of her clothes. "So how long do you think you were going to be able to lie about going to the hospital with Mary?"

"I uh, uh . . ."

"Uh-uh, my ass." She threw a stack of clothes at him. "She had the baby? And you were there with her?"

"Rachel, no, it's not like that. Please, let me explain."

She gave him a withering look. "There is nothing you can explain about the fact that you were with her as she had her baby! Then you stand here and lie to me about it! Give me one good reason why you would even think that I would be okay with you going to the hospital with that woman?"

"I didn't intend to go to the hospital with her."

"*I didn't intend to go to the hospital with her,*" Rachel said mockingly. "You didn't intend to go to the hospital, just like you didn't intend to get her pregnant. What did you intend to do, Lester?"

"Rachel, please just hear me out."

She ignored him as she pulled open another dresser drawer and began taking her clothes out and stuffing them in the suitcase.

"I'm tired of hearing your lies. I'm tired of this humiliating position you've placed me and our family in. The fact of the matter is, I have absolutely nothing to say to you except I'm done."

"Rachel . . ." He tried to approach her.

She raised her hands to keep him off. "Lester, I'm tired." Rachel fought back the tears that were threatening to fill her eyes. "It's bad enough that I had to deal with all these hateful, hypocritical people at the church. But I fought my way through it. Then you bring this mess to my doorstep, into my home. Still, I was expected to walk around with my head held high, being a proper First Lady, wondering all along if some other woman is carrying my husband's child. I did it. I fought my way through the pain and ridicule and torment from that woman." She dropped her hands wearily. "But I have no fight left. What woman in her right mind would be able to deal with all that I've been through?"

"I know it's been difficult," he said.

"You don't know a thing," she spat. "You don't know half of what I'm feeling. You knew how I felt about Bobby, but I chose you. I made the decision to give my marriage a try. Even though Bobby was in my ear telling me that we could make it work, I made the decision to give my all to you, and this is how you repay me?"

Lester's eyes started watering up as well. "So are you wishing you had gone with Bobby?" he asked solemnly.

"Uggghhh! This isn't about Bobby!" she screamed. "You don't need to be worried about Bobby. You need to be worried about Lester and the pain you have caused me, the pain you have brought to our family. And then on top of everything else, you just plunge the knife even deeper in me by going to the hospital with her to deliver her child?"

"Rachel, baby, please hear me out," Lester pleaded.

She resumed her packing. "Lester, I'm done hearing you out. Me and the kids are leaving."

Lester's head dropped in defeat. "No, no," he finally said. "Don't disrupt the children. I'll leave."

She stopped packing and closed her suitcase.

"That's the best thing I've heard you say all day. I'll give you twenty minutes to get your stuff and get out."

Chapter 19

Mary glanced out the peephole and felt her heart sink into her stomach. She couldn't do this. Not today.

"Hey," the voice on the other side of the door said. "I see your eyeball. Open this friggin' door."

Maybe if I ignore her she will just go away, Mary thought.

"I ain't going nowhere," the voice declared. "If you don't open this door, I will just stand out here for all your neighbors to see. Matter of fact, I think I'll entertain them. Oh, say can you seeeee," the voice began singing.

Mary leaned back against the door.

". . . by the dawwwwn's early light . . ."

Mary took a deep breath and swung the door open. "What do you want, Mother?"

"Hey, sweet pea."

Mary wouldn't quite call her mother a crack addict, even though she looked like one. No, heroin was her drug of choice. And meth, and Xanax, and just about every other drug but crack. Mary's eyes went where they always went when she saw her mother—to the crease of her arms. As usual, both arms were peppered with brown spots, showing years' worth of needle abuse.

"What, Mama?"

"I came to see my granddaughter," she announced.

Mary inhaled. "*Grandson,* Mama. I had a son."

"Whatever," she said, waving her off. "It's my first grandbaby and I want to see him." She marched inside.

"Mama, I've asked you not to contact me."

"You're my baby girl. How I'm not supposed to contact you?"

Mary sighed and shut the door. "How'd you get my address anyway?"

"Ummm, the Yellow Pages?"

"I'm not listed."

Her mother shrugged like she didn't even feel like lying. "That last Western Union had your address on it," she said casually.

Mary gritted her teeth. She'd specifically asked them not to include her address when she'd sent her mother some money. What idiot hadn't followed her instructions?

The therapist at one of her homes had told her she just had to let her mother go, but at the end of the day, Margaret Westerland was still her mother and Mary had no one else.

She was an only child, and her mother's only brother had died years ago.

"Mama, I sent the money to help you pay your bills, not for you to track me down."

"It ain't enough. Don't you know we're in a recession? That boy in the White House ain't done nothing to turn this country around."

" 'Boy'?"

"Oh, here you go. Don't tell me you're one of them politically correct folks. Just 'cause your baby's a mutt, don't be getting all sensitive," Margaret said.

"My son is not a mutt," Mary said forcefully.

"Dang." Her mother laughed. "You gonna bite my head off. I ain't saying that like it's a bad thing. I always been partial to half-breeds. You remember that dog I brought you—"

Mary cut her mother off. "What do you want, Mama?" She wasn't about to let her mother go down this fictitious memory lane she had created over the years. Her mother had never so much as bought her a stuffed dog. "I don't have any money. So if that's what you're after, you're wasting your breath."

Her mother looked annoyed. "Guess I'm just gonna have to get it from Craig then," she said.

"Craig? What are you doing talking to Craig?"

Ironically, that's how Mary had gotten back in touch with her mother after not hearing from her for eight years. Mary had been with her then-boyfriend Craig when he'd gone to make a delivery to a house where her mother and a bunch of other people had been shooting up meth. Margaret had immediately recognized Mary and started telling everyone about her "baby girl." It had been the most humiliating and heartbreaking moment of Mary's life.

"Oh, I saw Craig at this little spot I was at."

Mary didn't bother asking what kind of spot. "Is he still selling drugs to you?"

"Naw. Since you acted all funny about it, he won't do it. How you act all hoity-toity and you got a rap sheet a mile long is beyond me." She tsked.

Mary restrained herself from saying anything. Just another reason she didn't like having her mother around. The only thing Margaret had ever done for Mary, since giving birth, was bailing Mary out of jail. And she never hesitated to remind Mary about that or her criminal record. Forget the fact that it was all petty stuff—check fraud, theft, impersonating a public servant—Margaret brought it up every chance she got.

"Craig doesn't wanna make you mad," Margaret continued. "Plus, he says I don't ever like to pay."

She rubbed her arms, then leaned over the playpen. "Let me see my grandchild."

Mary instinctively grabbed her mother's arm. "Mama, I will say this again. When you get yourself together, I will more than welcome you into my life. Until then—"

"This is a nice place you got here," her mother said, jerking her arm away and wandering off. "Oooh, how much is that stereo worth?"

"Mama—"

"I'm just joking," she cackled. "I ain't gonna try and take

your stereo. But that iPod . . ." She pointed at the mp3 player on the coffee table. "Now, that's nice. Craig told me you got some kind of scam going on."

"I don't have any kind of scam going on," Mary said sternly. She hadn't talked to Craig since she'd first found out she was pregnant. He'd called to say hello and Mary had boldly told him that she was pregnant in hopes that he'd leave her alone. Of course, he'd started in with a whole bunch of questions about how far along she was and stuff like that. She'd finally had to tell him that it was this big-time preacher's baby. He'd been impressed and left her alone.

"Mm-hmm, *sure* you aren't scamming." Margaret winked. "I just want to make sure you take care of your mama."

"I repeat, I am not running a scam."

"Yeah, yeah," her mother said with a crazed smile. "Craig said you done hooked up with one of them mega preachers. T. D. Jakes or something. You getting it with T. D. Jakes?"

Mary headed toward the door. "Good-bye, Mama."

"Who's your baby's father?" she asked again. "Craig said he was married and had lots of money."

Her mother was the last person on earth she'd give any names to. "Can you just go? I'm not in the mood."

"Well, let Mama give you some advice. You'd better get what you can, while you can, because ain't none of these fools gonna care about you."

"Thank you very much for those insightful words." Mary held the door open for her mother to leave.

"All I know is if he is some type of mega preacher, you

better take him for what you can." Her mother walked toward the door. "'Cause when he figures out how low you are, he's gonna dump you so fast you won't know what hit you. Look at the way you treat your mama."

"Duly noted. Good-bye, Mother."

Margaret stopped in the doorway and held her hand out. "You're not gonna give me any money for real?"

Mary sighed. She hated being in the same room with her mother, and she knew the longer she fought her on anything, the longer it would take to get rid of her. "Hold on," she huffed as she stomped back into her bedroom. She sifted through her purse, pulled out a twenty-dollar bill, then made her way back into the living room. "This is all the money I have." She pushed the money into her mother's hand. "Now go and don't come back until you're clean."

Her mother broke out in a huge grin. "I'll get clean. I promise. Right after I go see a man about a dog."

Mary didn't reply as she hustled her mother out the door. She swallowed hard as she struggled not to cry. Her relationship with her mother had been a tumultuous one. For ten years Mary hadn't seen or heard from her. Then when Mary was fifteen, Margaret had reappeared, snatched Mary out of the one stable foster home she'd managed to live in, and moved her into their trailer. She'd paraded an array of men in and out all day long. Mary had been determined that that wouldn't be her life. She'd left home at seventeen and had been on her own ever since.

"Bye, bye, baby. I'll see you and my grandbaby around," Margaret said before bouncing down the stairs.

Mary slammed the door closed. "I will not let her get to me," she muttered to herself. She walked over to the playpen, picked up her baby, and kissed him gently on the head. "This is about you and me, baby. We will be one big happy family." She squeezed her son tightly, warmth filling her heart at the thought of what was to come. She looked over and noticed her mp3 player was gone. She was just about to get upset when she said, "You know what? Let her have it. You and me, sweetie, we're looking toward the future. The trailer trash past will soon be a distant memory. And you, my little one, will experience all the joy you deserve." Lester Jr. smiled at that very moment, as if to say he couldn't have agreed more.

Chapter 20

Jonathan looked up from his desk to see someone pacing back and forth outside his closed door. School was over and most of the teachers and students were gone, so he didn't know who it could be.

He peeked out the door just in time to see Roderick take off around the corner.

"Roderick?" Jonathan called.

Caught, Roderick stuck his head back around the corner. "Yeah, Mr. Jackson?"

"How are you doing?" Jonathan could tell the boy was uneasy, even though he was trying to fake a smile.

Roderick appeared fully around the corner. "I'm okay."

"You need to talk to me?"

Roderick put his hands in his pockets and looked down. "Ummm, no. I was . . . I was just hanging out."

Jonathan hadn't seen Roderick since the day his father had shown up. That was unusual, because he usually saw the boy in passing on a daily basis. It was almost as if he was purposely avoiding Jonathan. The principal had managed to calm Mr. Hurst down, but thankfully, he hadn't shifted the boy to a different counselor, as Mr. Hurst had wanted.

"Hanging out after school, by yourself?" Jonathan asked.

Roderick lowered his head and didn't respond.

"Well, you know what? I'd like to talk to you," Jonathan said. He motioned toward his office. "Why don't you come on in?"

Jonathan couldn't help but notice the look of relief pop up on Roderick's face as the boy walked past him and into the office.

"Have a seat." Jonathan bent down to the little refrigerator he kept under his desk. "Do you want a Coke?"

"Yeah. I mean, yes, sir, I'd like a Coke."

Jonathan took out a soda, handed it to Roderick, then reached in for another. He popped the top, took a sip, then sat down at his desk and studied Roderick. The boy showed no signs of initiating any conversation.

"So, how are things going?"

Roderick shrugged. "A'ight, I guess."

Jonathan sighed at the too-brief response, then decided to take a different approach. "You know, I'm in trouble myself."

Roderick's eyes grew wide. "You are? For what?"

"Well, I get paid to counsel people and no one has come in to talk to me lately, and my boss is wondering why they even need me. So, he may have to get rid of me."

Roderick flashed a "Yeah, right" smile.

Jonathan feigned innocence. "You don't want me to get fired, do you?"

"No, sir. You're one of the nicest counselors we have."

"So help me out then."

Roderick sighed, realizing he'd been tricked. "Well, I, umm . . ." He shut down before finishing his sentence.

"Is this about the guys bullying you?"

Roderick didn't answer.

"I know they give you a hard time," Jonathan continued.

"The only reason it's not worse is because of Rodney," Roderick said, finally opening up.

"Yeah, your brother does look out for you."

Roderick nodded solemnly. "He does, but I'm nothing but trouble for him."

Jonathan didn't like the sound of that. "What do you mean?"

"That's what my dad says. I even heard him telling his friend one time that he wishes I had never been born. He said he can't stand having a wimp for a son. He said I gave Hurst men a bad name." Roderick looked up sadly. "He thinks I'm gay, just like everybody else thinks, except Rodney. But I'm not," he protested. "I can't help it if I'm not strong and I don't like football or other stupid sports. But that doesn't mean I'm gay or gonna ever be gay."

"Do you have any interest in girls?" Jonathan asked.

Roderick shrugged nonchalantly. "Not really. But I don't have an interest in boys, either," he added. "And unlike my brother, I'm a virgin." He swallowed deeply. "Everybody thinks there's something wrong with that. Honestly, I just wanna wait until I'm married. But I don't even tell people that because that makes me some kind of freak or something, or as my dad says, 'like a queer.'"

Jonathan was so proud of Roderick. Proud and sad. Here this boy was trying to do the right thing, and he was being ridiculed and ostracized, and his own father was leading the pack.

"What do you have an interest in?" Jonathan asked. Maybe if he could help Roderick focus on the things that really mattered, Roderick could get rid of that emptiness in his eyes.

"Art," Roderick replied with a wide smile. "I want to be an artist, like Monet." His expression quickly changed. "I told my dad that one time and he went ballistic."

Jonathan's heart went out to Roderick. He could only imagine what the boy must have been going through.

"And I don't understand it," Roderick continued. "Monet was married and had a woman on the side," he said, shaking his head. "Even Jacob Lawrence—that's a contemporary African-American artist—was married."

It was obvious he was passionate about art. The sad part was, no one had probably ever nurtured his talent.

"My daddy wants me to be like Rodney." Roderick was on a roll. He seemed to be relieved to be getting so much off his chest. "Rodney has a whole bunch of girlfriends. But they just want him because they think he's gonna go pro and make a whole lot of money one day. My dad says something is wrong with a"—he made air quotes with his hands—"hot-blooded teenager who doesn't like girls." Roderick sighed in defeat. "Maybe my blood isn't hot yet. Maybe I just haven't found that special someone. But believe me, Mr. Jackson, it's not gonna be a boy. Only, these days you have to be either or. If you don't like girls, you must like boys, as my dad always says."

Jonathan could relate to everything Roderick was saying. And the fact that Rodney was so athletic only served to hammer home Roderick's feeling of inferiority. Jonathan had seen firsthand how living in someone's athletic shadow could take its toll. David had been a superstar football player, heading for the pros until an injury his sophomore year of college had ended his career. He'd dropped out of college and taken two-bit jobs until he'd hooked up with his girlfriend Tawny and became addicted to drugs. But all during childhood everyone had wanted to know why Jonathan hadn't been as athletic as his legendary brother.

"My dad says he's going to kill me if Rodney loses his football scholarship because of me."

"If Rodney loses anything, it will be his own doing," Jonathan quickly put in.

Roderick vehemently shook his head. "No, because he wouldn't be fighting if he didn't always have to take up for me. I don't want my brother to lose out on going to college because of me," he said plaintively. "I just want to live my life and I want everybody to leave me alone."

"Have you tried talking to your parents?"

Roderick released a pained laugh. "Yeah, right."

Unfortunately, Jonathan knew that feeling as well. "Do you want me to talk to your parents?"

Roderick's eyes widened in horror. "Oh, no! I'm telling you, there is no getting through to my dad. You going to talk to him will only make things worse."

Jonathan nodded in understanding.

"I guess I just needed to vent. And for some reason I feel like you get me," Roderick said.

Maybe they were kindred spirits, Jonathan thought. Maybe Roderick could feel that Jonathan understood his pain. The problem was, he didn't know how he could help.

"It's crazy," Roderick said forlornly. "My brother is the biggest playa when it comes to girls. Don't get me wrong, I love him, but he's a playa for real. He runs girls left and right. And my dad thinks that's cool. He's always patting him on the back and telling me I need to be more like him. Really, I think my brother only does it because he knows it makes my dad happy. 'Cause he's not like that, really. He doesn't like hurting people. But he plays it all the way because he knows the girls and football are the only things that truly make my dad happy." Roderick lowered his head in shame. "I've accepted that I can never make him happy," he said sadly.

Jonathan had heard enough. "You know what?" he said. "Why don't you try to make yourself happy? What would make you happy?"

A sad smile returned to Roderick's face. "Art school. Like if

I could get a scholarship, I could go away. Far, far away. Maybe even another country, a boarding school or something, where I can draw and draw and draw."

"Well, you know you still have to take your core classes," Jonathan cautioned.

"That's fine, I can learn that stuff, too. But just as long as I can draw and grow as an artist and not worry about people judging me."

"Tell you what," Jonathan said as an idea suddenly came to him, "I don't know about another country. But why don't I look up some information on art schools and then we could sit down and talk about your future?"

At last that brought a smile to the boy's eyes. "I'd like that," Roderick said. He rose to his feet. "I knew there was a reason I came to talk to you."

"Well, I'm glad you did." Jonathan stood also and began walking him to the door. "And thank you for saving my job. I owe you. Can I get an Obama bump?" Jonathan held up his fist.

Roderick smiled proudly as he bumped fists with Jonathan.

"You come see me any time you need anything."

"Thank you," Roderick said as he slung his backpack over his shoulder and headed out.

Jonathan was so pleased to see Roderick's delight at the idea of art school. Maybe he could help the boy, after all. Since he couldn't help himself, maybe he could help someone else.

Jonathan gathered up his things, then headed out to his car. He was tired and ready to go home, but knew he needed to go check on his father. He pulled out his cell phone and dialed his father's number.

"Hey, Brenda," he said when his stepmom picked up.

"Hi, Jonathan. How are you?"

"Fine. Is my dad there?"

"Of course. You want me to get him for you?"

"Nah, I was just going to swing by, but, um, ah . . ."

She laughed. "Your aunt isn't here. She's at the hospital visiting her friend."

Jonathan smiled. "Good. I'm on my way."

Twenty minutes later, Jonathan sat on the sofa across from his father. They chatted for a while, about last night's game, the presidential race, and Rachel and Lester's drama. Finally, Simon said, "Okay, son, do you want to tell me the real reason you're here? I can tell something's eating at you."

Jonathan was surprised that his father was in tune with him. That had always been his mother's talent. For most of his life, Loretta had been the one who'd known when something had been eating at Jonathan, while Simon had remained oblivious to everything.

Jonathan debated whether he should even say something about what was really on his mind. On the drive over he'd thought about Roderick, and what Mr. Hurst had said. Maybe Roderick was just an effeminate young man with no interest in girls. But if he was genuinely confused about his sexuality, he didn't need anyone influencing him, because this lifestyle was hard. Jonathan wanted to make sure nothing he did or said could influence the teen one way or the other.

The whole train of thought led him back to his own childhood, how he'd had the same feelings as Roderick from a very young age. His failure to act on them, then his decision *to* act, had caused nothing but misery in his life.

He knew he could never have that conversation with his father, but his dad could advise him on one area.

"Dad, do you believe you can pray away gayness?" Jonathan quietly asked. It was the first time in years that he'd even broached the subject with his father. They had a sort of "don't ask, don't tell" policy in their family.

Simon struggled to mask his discomfort. "Son . . ."

"We don't have to talk about me. Just in general."

Simon leaned back in his seat, thinking carefully about his response. "You're my son and I will always love you," he began. "I don't understand this phase you're going through."

Jonathan didn't know why his father continued to talk about his sexuality as a phase, but he didn't touch that topic. "I just need to know, do you think you can pray away the gay?" Jonathan said.

"I know that God can deliver us from anything. Anything," Simon said with firmness.

"But what does that mean?"

Simon shook his head as he pursed his lips. "Jon, I can't talk about this. I can accept who you say you are—I don't like it, but I can accept you. However, I can never sit here and hold a conversation with you about it. You know how I feel. You know what the Word says. You were raised in the Word."

"But the Word says a lot of things. Why do people only

take this part of the Bible to hammer home the most?" Jonathan knew his father was uncomfortable, but he was really seeking some answers.

He wasn't going to get any. "Son, I'm glad you stopped by. Make sure you bring Chase this weekend." Simon pulled himself up out of the recliner. "I'm really tired and I'm gonna go upstairs and lay down."

Jonathan sat back, defeated. He didn't know why he'd thought he'd get anywhere with his dad. Now, more than ever, he knew exactly how Roderick felt.

Chapter 21

Rachel turned over for what had to be the twentieth time. She glanced blearily at the digital alarm clock on her nightstand. It was three thirty in the morning, and she was going on her fourth sleepless night. She had shed more tears in the last four days than she had in the last four years. *It has to be the hormones,* she told herself. She was stressed out about Lester, her kids kept asking questions that she wasn't ready to answer, and everybody was blowing up her phone.

Rachel was so thankful that Brenda had come and gotten the children. She'd told Rachel to take her time and figure out what she wanted to do. She would make sure the kids were transported back and forth to school every day. After the first day of pleading and begging, Lester had finally given her her space. He must've realized that he would do better by just leaving her alone. The crazy part was Rachel felt an emptiness now that Lester wasn't around. She actually missed him, and she had started giving him the benefit of the doubt. He wouldn't blatantly go to Mary's side, would he? Not after all they'd been through. Maybe he really had been trying to get her to leave the church like he'd said, then something had happened.

"Ugggh," Rachel said, rolling back the covers and pulling her heavy frame up out of the bed. She had three more weeks to go and she couldn't get comfortable for anything in this world. Maybe a cup of hot chamomile tea would help her sleep. She didn't bother reaching for her robe as she made her way downstairs.

Rachel had put on the hot water when a sharp pain jabbed her in the side. She screamed in agony as the pain deepened and then quickly subsided.

She was just about to take a deep breath when she looked down to notice the puddle of water at her feet.

"Oh my God, please tell me this is not happening," she muttered as she felt the water trickle down her leg.

Rachel gripped the wall as she made her way over to the cordless phone. She picked it up and punched in Jonathan's number. He lived closest to her and had ordered that she call him in the event anything happened. He actually wanted to stay with her until she figured out what she was going to do, but Rachel wasn't hearing it. Besides, both of her other kids had been past due, so she'd never dreamed she'd go into labor three weeks early.

Now, as another jolt of pain shot through her stomach, she regretted the decision. These didn't resemble her other contractions. These had come out of nowhere and were picking up in pace.

"Jonathan?" she said when he answered.

"Rachel? What's wrong?"

"My, my . . . my water broke." Another pain shot through her stomach. She couldn't believe that she was in her home alone. What in the world had she been thinking? What if the baby started coming?

"Okay, okay," Jonathan said.

"I don't want to have my baby alone," she cried.

"Rachel, calm down," Jonathan said. "You're not going to have your baby alone." She heard rumbling, and his voice became muffled.

"I can't hear you!" she screamed.

More rumbling, then, "I'm sorry, I was getting out of bed and throwing my clothes on. I said, you won't have your baby by yourself. I am on my way and will be there in twenty minutes."

"What if my baby won't wait twenty minutes?"

Rachel suddenly had a disturbing thought. She didn't know her neighbors' phone numbers. She used to know the family to the left of her, but they had moved and the house was empty. The family on the other side pretty much kept to themselves. Now, when she needed someone, she didn't know whom to call.

"Jonathan, please hurry."

"I'm out the door now," he said. "Do you want me to call 9-1-1?"

Rachel took a deep breath. She could do this. "I'll wait. If the contractions come any faster, I'll call. But hurry."

"All right. I'm going to hang up and call David and see where he is. Then I'm going to call you back and stay on the phone with you until I get there, so answer, okay?"

"Okay." Rachel hung up the phone, then set it down on the floor next to her. She felt herself calming down, everything was all right—and then she let out another scream. She didn't remember the pain being as intense with her other children. Yes, she'd been a lot younger then, but age shouldn't make this much of a difference, should it?

Dear God, please don't let me have my baby on the kitchen floor. Please let me make it to the hospital.

Rachel was pulling herself up to wait by the door for Jonathan when she heard the front door chime, signaling someone was entering the house. Maybe Jonathan had gotten in touch with David. *But how did he get in?* she wondered.

Rachel was just about to call out to him when she heard Lester's voice. "Rachel, honey, where are you?"

She hurried to the living room doorway. "What are you doing here?"

"Come on," he said, immediately coming to her aid. "I'm taking you to the hospital."

Although she was in pain, Rachel jerked away from him. "What are you doing here?" she repeated.

"I couldn't stand the thought of you being alone when

you're so close to the delivery," he explained. "So I've been sleeping in the car down the street. I told Jonathan to call me immediately if you needed me."

"Well, I don't nee— Ahhhhhh!" Rachel doubled over as another contraction kicked her insides.

"Rachel, just breathe, baby." Lester guided her toward the doorway. "Is your bag still in the closet?"

He didn't give her time to answer but headed straight to the closet. He'd made her pack it a month ago.

"Come on." When she seemed reluctant to go with him, he added, "You can curse me out after you have a safe delivery."

Rachel was no longer in the mood to protest. Honestly, she was thankful that he was here. For tonight at least, she would put aside any anger and focus all of her attention on delivering a healthy baby.

Chapter 22

Rachel stared down at the bundle of joy nestled in her arms. Her baby girl was so adorable. She had Lester's sandpaper coloring and reddish brown hair. But everything else about her was the spitting image of Rachel.

"Hey, the nurse needs to take the baby for some more testing," Lester said, approaching the bedside. He looked unsure, as if he was still worried about whether he was welcome.

Rachel was so exhausted that she didn't have the energy to let any negativity reside in her space.

"Isn't she precious?" Rachel asked.

"She is," Lester said, regarding the baby lovingly. "Just like her mother." He swallowed, then waited patiently as the nurse took the baby out. Once she was gone, he went on. "Look, I'm sorry I was sitting outside the house. I don't want you to think

I'm a stalker or anything, but I was really concerned about you being alone so close to the due date. I—"

Rachel held up a hand to cut him off. "I'm glad you were there." She shifted, trying to ease some of the pain shooting through her abdomen. "Did you talk to my dad?"

"Yes, Brenda told me to call when we were ready for her to bring up the kids. I figured we'd let you get a little rest, then we'd let them in. You know they're dying to meet their brand-new sister."

Rachel stretched as she tried to no avail to get comfortable.

"You should get up and walk."

She cut her eyes at him. When they'd arrived at the hospital, they'd had to do an emergency C-section because the cord had been wrapped around the baby's neck. Rachel had never wanted a C-section because, in her mind, real women delivered their babies naturally. But with all the pain she'd been enduring, that mentality had gone out the window. All she'd wanted to do was deliver a healthy baby.

"Knock, knock. Can I come in?" Twyla stuck her head in the door. She was carrying a stuffed teddy bear with a bunch of balloons.

"Hey, girl," Rachel said.

"How's the mommy?" Twyla asked. "Hi, Lester."

"Hi, Twyla," Lester replied.

"Hey, girl. What are you doing here so soon?" Rachel asked.

"Girl, please, as soon as Lester called me, I came."

Rachel glanced over at Lester and her heart momentarily

warmed. Despite everything they'd been through, Lester always took care of her. Between waiting outside the house and making sure everyone was notified, he'd made sure things were taken care of. That was one of the things she had always loved about him.

"Well, if you two will excuse me, I'm going to go stand outside the nursery and idolize my baby," Lester said, interrupting her thoughts.

As soon as the door closed, Twyla said, "First of all, how are you feeling?"

"I'm fine. The baby is precious, of course."

Twyla excitedly sat down in the chair next to the bed. "Okay then, secondly, tell me, what is he doing here? I mean, not that I'm knocking it, because I think it's great that he was here for the delivery of the baby, but when I talked to you last night, you were going to bed alone."

Rachel reached for the glass of ice water on her nightstand and took a sip. "Girl, don't even get me started. Do you know, he was sleeping in the car outside of the house because he was scared I was going to go into labor? He's been there for the last four nights."

"Wow," Twyla said. "But you know what, it doesn't surprise me."

Rachel turned up her lip. "Yeah, whatever." She didn't want to admit how touched she was by the gesture.

"I know you don't want to hear this, but Lester is a good guy."

"I didn't know they changed the definition of 'good' to men who cheat on their wives and possibly get another woman pregnant."

"Well, I don't condone that at all, but I'm just saying we all make mistakes."

"Whatever, Twyla."

"Besides, by kicking Lester out, you're letting her win, and the Rachel I know would never let anybody else win."

Rachel sat up a little straighter. "What does that mean?"

"It means," Twyla said, "I can understand you not being able to accept this baby once it's proven to be his. But I can't understand how you're going to just give up without all the facts."

"The fact remains that he was with her when she delivered her baby."

"And he was with you when you delivered yours. And was he sleeping with you at the time?" she pointed out. "No. All I'm saying is hear him out. You know the whole way they got together was set up. She preyed on his weakness. And again, I'm not condoning it. He messed up bad and trust me, you've more than made him pay." She ignored the storm gathering in Rachel's eyes. "Look, we both know that's not his baby. It's just more of her conniving."

"Yeah, I've thought about that . . ."

"What will you do if you run him off, throw away this marriage, then you find out that it's not his, that it was all part of some sick, twisted game Mary was playing?"

"Oh, it wouldn't be pretty." Just the thought set Rachel's blood to boiling.

"I know, so why give her the satisfaction? If the baby turns out to be his, then you deal with it. If that means you leave, you'll be all right. I'll be there to help you with the baby. Your whole family will. But just wait and see."

Rachel hadn't considered the problem from that angle. "I'll think about it," she sighed as the nurse wheeled the baby back into the room. Twyla immediately picked her up.

"What's her name anyway?"

"Brooklyn. Brooklyn Lorraine Adams."

Twyla was waggling her finger at the infant's face. "I like that."

"Me, too, that's why I chose it."

"Well, all I'm saying," Twyla said, getting back to the point, "is let Lester come home. Let him take care of you and try your best to start rebuilding your family."

Rachel weighed her friend's words. Was she letting Mary win by giving up? The more she thought about it, the more she decided that Twyla was right. She was Rachel Jackson Adams. A strong, fighting woman. And she'd be damned if this tramp sent her slithering away. No, Mary had awakened the old Rachel, and if Mary thought she could snatch Rachel's man, then she'd better think again.

Chapter 23

The light tapping on his closed office door caused Jonathan to look up from his computer.

"Come in," he said.

The door opened and Roderick stuck his head in the office. "Hey, Mr. Jackson. Mrs. Poe said you wanted to see me."

Jonathan smiled and motioned for the boy to come in. He was carrying his backpack and a large black art case. He wore an Ed Hardy T-shirt and some baggy jeans.

"Come on in. Have a seat." Jonathan pulled a manila folder out of his drawer and slid it toward Roderick. "I got some info on art schools." He smiled as Roderick's eyes lit up. Roderick had dropped off some of his drawings and they were actually good. That made Jonathan even more determined to help.

"Wow, thanks, Mr. Jackson!" Roderick took the folder and

pulled out the papers as he slid into the chair in front of Jonathan's desk.

Jonathan motioned to the first sheet. He had planned to just give the boy the papers and send him on his way, but his excitement was contagious. "That's the Rhode Island School of Design," Jonathan continued. "It's a very prestigious school, and I think you could not only get in but you could also get a scholarship. The problem is, the deadline is in a couple of weeks and you need a portfolio. Do you have anything?"

"Of course, I have all kinds of stuff." Roderick read the paper. "But what's this observational art and personal art stuff they say I have to submit?"

"Well, apparently, observational art is a drawing of a model, portrait or landscape, and personal art is more an example of your unique interests."

Roderick lost his smile. "I have some personal stuff, but I've never done a model or landscape."

"Well, it sounds like you need to get to it, then."

Roderick grinned widely again. "Cool. I was . . . um, never mind."

"No, what were you about to say?"

Roderick hesitated, then giddily continued. "I was telling Benjamin about art school—you know he's an artist, too, that's why we were talking the other day, about art stuff. And he was talking about how good my drawings were and he offered to help me because he's already been accepted to DeVry."

Jonathan cringed. He didn't want to encourage Roderick's relationship with Benjamin. That would only lead to more problems that Roderick couldn't handle. Jonathan almost said something, but he stopped himself. What if Benjamin was straight? he wondered. Would this be an issue? But what if Benjamin was like Tracy, the young man who had introduced Jonathan to "life on the other side," as he used to call it? Jonathan had been in college, an age when he'd been able to make a rational decision, so he'd known what he'd been getting into. Roderick was too young to face issues like that.

"What's wrong, Mr. Jackson?" Roderick asked.

Jonathan shook his thoughts away. No, he didn't need to bring sexuality into this. These were two high school students who shared a common passion for art. He was not going to let his own personal demons guide his advice.

"N-nothing's wrong," Jonathan said, plastering on a grin. "I'm just glad you're happy. I really think you'll get in."

Roderick slid the papers back in the folder, then stood. "Thank you so much, Mr. Jackson. You just don't know how much this means to me. And I'll have my drawing done asap!"

Jonathan couldn't help but smile. For the first time he had seen Roderick happy, and if art brought him that joy, then they were definitely on the right track.

Chapter 24

"Hey, sweet thang." Mary didn't have to turn around to know who that voice belonged to. She couldn't believe he would have the nerve to show up at her apartment.

"Craig, what are you doing here?" she said, turning to face him. He must've been waiting outside her apartment complex while she'd taken her baby for a walk.

"Well, since you won't return my phone calls and you want to act all high society on me now, well, you didn't leave me much choice, now, did you?" He reached out and stroked her cheek. His touch gave her goose bumps, but not in a good way. She wrenched away from him like he disgusted her.

"Oh, so it's like that now?" he said, watching her reaction. He looked the same, wearing sagging blue jeans and a skimpy muscle shirt, which exposed his sculpted biceps. He'd cut off his signature braids, but it looked like he was trying to let them grow back out.

"Craig, I'll ask you again, why are you here?"

He pointed at her apartment and frowned. "This isn't what I expected. Since you bagged a big-time preacher, well," he looked around the apartment complex, "I thought he would've set you up better than this."

She put her hands on her hips. "I don't need anyone to set me up. I can take care of myself."

Craig stared at her, then burst out laughing. "Girl, you can still act." He motioned toward her door. "Come on, aren't you going to invite me in?"

"And why would I do that?"

"Because I want to talk to you. And I want to see your precious little boy. I heard he was super cute."

"He is and I wouldn't let you anywhere near my son." She scooted the stroller behind her.

His eyes bugged out in pretend awe. "*Your* son, huh?"

"Yes, mine and *Lester Adams*'s, Reverend Lester Adams."

Craig doubled over in laughter. "I never pictured you to be a preacher's woman." He let the laugh work its way out. "But wait, you're not," he added with a wry smile.

"Shut up, Craig." She tried to push her way past him and go inside.

He shifted more in front of her. "Now, you know I did my homework."

"A good crook always does."

"You didn't call me a crook when you were running game

156

with me." He smiled at her slyly. "We were so good together. Bonnie and Clyde."

Mary groaned in exasperation. They'd run all kinds of scams, from identity theft to check scams to insurance fraud. But that was then. This was now.

"Well, that was before you took crime to another level. Besides, those days are long gone," Mary said. She pointed to her stroller. "As you can see, I'm a changed woman."

He gave the baby an arched eyebrow. "Naw, girl, it looks to me like you just got a new game," he said coolly.

"Whatever, Craig. This isn't a game."

"So, do you really think you stand a chance with preacher man?"

"For your information, I do."

"And what about his wife and kids?"

"A mere formality." She wondered how Craig knew all of her business, but then again, this was Craig she was talking about. He could find out anything about anyone.

He leaned against the doorway, his expression turning serious.

"Mary, what do you want with a preacher?"

"Stability, a real life. Not to have to worry about how I'm gonna keep the lights on or how I'm gonna send my kid to college. I don't want to be scared to open the front door because I'm afraid the cops are coming to bust me and my man. You know, all the things you couldn't give me."

"Let's just say for argument's sake that you were even able to weasel preacher man away from his family. Do you really think you'd be happy in the boring, humdrum life as a First Lady in a black church?"

"What difference does color make?"

He shook his head in pity. "My poor Mary, always so naive. Sweetheart, just 'cause you want a color-blind world doesn't mean it exists. Just like white folks can be racist against blacks, blacks can be racist against whites, especially when you start messing with their religion."

She had already experienced some of that, but she wouldn't admit it. "Craig, I'm through talking to you." She opened the door and navigated the stroller inside.

He put his foot in the door to keep her from closing it. "You didn't even ask me what I wanted."

"It doesn't matter."

"Let me hold a couple of dollars."

She stopped and cocked her head. "You are the brokest con man I've ever seen."

"Hey, times are hard, haven't you heard? Besides, I have a plan that's about to set me on easy street. I just need a few hundred dollars to hold me over until then."

"A couple of dollars and a few hundred dollars are two different things," she said with an edge. "But it doesn't matter anyway, because I don't have any money."

"But you got a so-called baby by a preacher. That ought to be worth something."

"What the hell do you mean so-called baby by a preacher?"

"Okay, that came out wrong."

Mary cut him off. She wasn't about to go tit for tat with

Craig. It was bad enough her mom had come begging, now Craig was doing the same thing.

"Look, I don't have any money. Lester isn't paying me any child support yet. I have to take him to court, which I'm trying to avoid because I know he'll do right. I just have to give him time. And when he does pay, it's for my son and my son only."

"Your son," he said again with a laugh.

"Yes, *my* son," she stressed, pushing the stroller behind her.

"All right, baby." He paused, licking his lips. "You sure I can't come in? You know, a romp for old times' sake?"

"I'm positive. Bye, Craig."

He leaned in and kissed her on the cheek. "Bye, babe. Until next time." He leaned down and looked into the stroller. Lester was sound asleep. "Bye, lil man." Craig turned his attention back to Mary. "I hope you know what you're doing."

"I do," she said, her face stony.

"All right." He broke out in a big smile again. "I'll be in touch."

As Mary watched him walk away, she felt a sinking feeling in her stomach. Whenever Craig was around, trouble wasn't too far behind.

Chapter 25

Although Rachel hadn't wanted to come to the church picnic, she was now glad that she had. This was her first outing with the baby, and they truly felt like a family. Brooklyn was covered up and sitting in her car seat. Nia and Jordan were running around the park. And Lester was acting like father of the year. To anyone looking on, they would seem like the All-American family, and for the last week, they'd felt like one, too.

Rachel had been pleasantly surprised not to have heard from Mary in the past six weeks. Maybe Lester had gotten through to her. He'd explained to Rachel what he'd been doing with Mary the night she'd gone into labor. Maybe the fact that Rachel had had her baby too had brought Mary to her senses and she'd leave them alone. Maybe, but somehow Rachel doubted it. In fact, not hearing from Mary was making her even more uneasy. The fact that she hadn't tried to contact Lester in the last six weeks only meant that she was up to something.

Stop looking for trouble where it doesn't exist. She could almost hear her mother's voice. When Loretta had been alive, she'd always asked Rachel to settle down and "stop looking for trouble because you're likely to find it."

Rachel smiled at the memory. Her mom had been right. Rachel would simply enjoy today because she didn't know what tomorrow held.

Lester smiled at his wife as he walked up. He'd put the last of the food in the car. Almost everyone had left the picnic, and those who were left—Twyla, some members from the picnic committee and a few deacons—were cleaning up the park.

"Mommy, Mommy." Nia came rushing over to her. Loretta's old, crippled dog, Brandy, was trying to keep up. "Look what I got." She held up a giant multicolored round lollipop.

Rachel immediately stiffened. "Where'd you get that?"

"From that lady over there." Nia pointed back toward the other side of the park. "The one you were fighting with at church." Rachel's stomach churned at the sight of Mary.

"Lester . . ." Rachel didn't have to say a word. Lester's gaze was already trained across the park.

"This woman is certifiable," Rachel muttered as she pulled herself up off the ground. "And I've had enough."

Before Lester could blink, Rachel was stomping over toward Mary. "Look, you stalking psycho—"

"Well, look at the Adams family," Mary quipped. She called

out to Lester, who was hurrying over as well. "Can your son come meet his siblings?" She gently rocked the stroller.

"Mary, I told you, if the baby is mine, I'm going to pay child support," Lester said as he approached them.

The words made Rachel cringe. Yes, she was working through her issues, but no way would she be able to forgive Lester if that baby turned out to be his. He'd told Rachel that until Mary had a DNA test, he would have no more contact with her.

"The baby is yours. How many times do I have to tell you that?" Mary said with the utmost confidence.

"If you're so sure, then you should have no problem taking a DNA test," Rachel demanded. "And I am tired of going back and forth with you on this. We don't want anything else to do with you or your kid until you submit to a DNA test."

A slow smile crept across her face. "Lester, sweetie, did you tell your wife that there is no need for a DNA test?"

"What? Of course there's a need for a DNA test. I have been very clear with you about that."

"Why do I need a DNA test when I have this?" She reached down into the baby's diaper bag and pulled out a sheet of paper. She thrust it at Rachel, who hesitated before snatching it.

"Acknowledgment of Paternity," Rachel read. She looked back at Mary. "And? What does this have to do with anything?"

Mary leaned in and pointed to the last line. "What does that say?"

"Mother Mary Richardson, father Lester Ad . . ." Rachel's voice trailed off as she noticed her husband's name and signature. She wanted to say that it was forged, but the L was looped in that fancy way that she always teased Lester about.

"You signed this?" Rachel asked Lester, shock registering on her face.

"Yes, but—"

"You acknowledged paternity?" Rachel repeated.

"He sure did," Mary taunted. "Because he knows the truth."

Lester stepped toward Rachel. "No, it's not like that at all. She made me sign."

"Oh, okay, I get it. She put a gun to your head and made you sign it!"

Mary reached down and tickled her baby. "You hear that, little Lester? Your daddy is so silly."

Rachel stared at her husband in disbelief. "She named this baby *Lester*?" Even as she said the words, her heart dropped into her stomach.

"I named him after his daddy," Mary said confidently as she picked the baby up.

Rachel was about to haul off and slap her again, but she caught herself. No, she had to leave before she lost her mind. "Go to hell, Mary." Rachel spun around and started walking off.

Lester took off after her. "Rachel, baby, let me explain," he said, reaching out and grabbing her arm.

Rachel snatched her arm away. "Lester . . ." She noticed Mary standing off to the side. She was delighted they were fighting.

"What?" Mary said, shifting her baby in her arms. "Don't let me stop you. I'm just—"

Rachel didn't give her a chance to finish as she turned and stormed off. She'd dealt with all that she could deal with. Baby or no baby, this was the absolute last straw.

She stomped past Twyla and Nia, who looked terrified. "I'm sorry, Mommy. I shouldn't have taken the candy. I'll give it back."

Rachel didn't say anything as she kept walking.

"Rachel, what's the matter with you?" Twyla said, running to catch up with her.

Rachel rounded the corner, then leaned against the pavilion wall. "I don't want to talk about it."

"No, you're going to tell me what's wrong," Twyla demanded. "What did Mary want?"

"This tramp is stalking me now." She covered her eyes and started crying. "Why won't she leave us alone?"

"No, ma'am," Twyla said, her mouth agape. "Who are you and what have you done with my friend?"

Rachel sniffed. "What are you talking about?"

"I'm talking about this," Twyla said, looking all around Rachel. "This crying and whining. The Rachel I know would never run off into a corner to cry."

"I can't take this," Rachel complained. "How much can I be expected to endure?"

"As much as necessary if that person is Rachel Jackson Adams." Twyla folded her arms. "I need you to go find your backbone. Fight back. Don't let her harass you *and* take your man."

Rachel sniffed. "She can have him."

"You don't mean that." Twyla softened her tone. "Look, I understand you're angry, and I understand that Lester needs his butt kicked, but you and me both know he's extremely remorseful, and out of all the men in the world who I would be willing to bet has learned their lesson, Lester is one of them."

Rachel wiped her eyes. "So what do you suggest I do?"

"Fight back."

"How?"

"I don't know. Just get your spunk back. You have always been a don't-get-mad-get-even type of girl." Rachel started to nod. She was right about that. "Yeah, I understand you have to change your ways because you're a First Lady," Twyla added, "but that doesn't mean you have to sit back and become some weak little wallflower."

"Oh, so now I'm weak?" Rachel tried to manage a laugh.

Twyla shook her friend. "No, you're not. That's what I'm trying to remind you. But right now you're letting her win. I mean, have you even run a background check on her?"

Rachel was struck by that suggestion. She hadn't. She really was slipping. She should've done a background check, a credit check, whatever was necessary. She'd done everything under the sun to get rid of Shante, and Bobby had just been her boyfriend. Why wasn't she fighting just as hard for her husband?

"Dust off that bag of tricks, girl," Twyla said, winking at her. "Do what you gotta do."

Say Amen, Again

Rachel managed a smile at her friend. She was right. It was time to stop whining and fight back. Really fight back. Rachel stood, brushed her shirt down, then held her head high. "You're right. I'm going to do what I have to do."

Rachel didn't know what that was. Yet she would bet that someone as nasty as Mary would have a few skeletons in her past. And now Rachel was on a mission to dig them up.

Chapter 26

Jonathan stood outside the door of the "Straight Talk" meeting. This was ridiculous, he told himself. You couldn't pray away gay. This was who he was. Whether God made him that way, or he turned that way, or what, Jonathan wasn't sure. All he did know was that this was a daily struggle. *But what if it's a struggle that can be overcome?* He heard his dad's voice say *"God can deliver us from anything."* He'd been raised to believe in the power of prayer, and Lord knows, he'd been praying like crazy for a resolution to the way he felt.

Jonathan took a deep breath, then pushed the door open. He found a group of people sitting around in a circle, and it immediately brought to mind a Narcotics Anonymous meeting he'd attended with David several years ago. Was being gay an addiction that he needed to fight?

Of the twenty people in the room, the majority of them were effeminate-looking men, but there were two stocky guys who looked like they could play professional football. There were also four women—one young woman, two elderly women, and perched in the middle of them was his aunt Minnie.

Jonathan had had no idea she would be here. That was the last thing he needed. He was just about to hightail it out of there when a man sitting at the front of the room motioned for him to come on in.

"Excuse me, Melvin," the man said, cutting off one of the effeminate men who was talking. "Come on in, we don't bite," he told Jonathan. Everyone turned to stare at him. Jonathan expected his aunt to say something, but she didn't say a word. She probably didn't want anyone to know they were related.

That was just fine with Jonathan. He took the only available seat, the one next to Melvin, which meant he would be right in the center of attention.

"I'm Vincent, the group leader. Feel free to jump in at any time," the man said, before motioning for Melvin to continue.

Jonathan was grateful Vincent didn't ask him to introduce himself. He didn't want any of these people knowing anything about him. He had come just to see . . . well, he wasn't sure why he was here.

Melvin dramatically cleared his throat. He was one of those types that gave gay men a bad name—over the top, hair slicked down, a Burberry scarf around his neck, Skinny jeans—and the way he used his hands to emphasize everything he said told the entire world that he was a drama queen. "Well," Melvin continued, "I wish everyone would stop acting like all you have to do is say a couple of Hail Mary's and you're cured."

One of the elderly ladies tsked. "Well, I have a cousin who was gay and he prayed, and everybody we know prayed, and glory be to Jesus, one day he was delivered. He is no longer gay," she said proudly.

"What's his name?" Melvin asked, doubtful.

"Levi Donalson. He's a walking testament." She nodded her head triumphantly.

"Umph, that's what I thought," Melvin said with a wide leer. He leaned over and whispered to Jonathan, "He tried to pick me up in a club last week."

Jonathan remained expressionless. He wasn't trying to make friends. He merely wanted to observe.

The group went back and forth, debating on whether you could pray the gay away. Finally Vincent turned to Jonathan and asked, "Do you have anything you'd like to say?"

"Ummm, I'm just here to listen," Jonathan replied.

"Well, we really like for everyone to join in the conversation," Vincent said.

"I . . . I don't know what to say," Jonathan said.

"Why don't you tell us what you think about Melvin's last statement?" Melvin had emphatically declared that this whole group was useless because you couldn't pray gay away. Jonathan had wanted to ask him what he was doing there if he thought that, but he'd let it go.

"Seriously, don't be ashamed. We all have our reasons for being here, so no one will stand in judgment of you," Vincent said.

Jonathan eyed the elderly women, who shifted their eyes away when Vincent made that statement. Minnie, however, curled her lip with utter disgust. That simple reaction made him recall every foul thing she had ever said. He thought back to all the hateful people at his church. But he also remembered what his mother had told him, that God's love was all-encompassing.

"Well," Jonathan began, "I don't think being gay is going to keep me out of Heaven, but it's my cross to bear here on earth."

"Amen," Melvin said.

"Besides," echoed another man who wore a name tag with the name Carl scrawled on it, "aren't you church folks the ones who claim that God forgives all sins? Why can't I be who I am and just ask for God's forgiveness if He thinks it's so wrong?"

"Lord Jesus," muttered one of the elderly women, who Jonathan recognized as the white-haired lady that had shown up at his house with his aunt.

"What, Miss Eula?" Carl said. "You don't think God can forgive me?"

She shook her head. "You can't just say, 'Now I lay me down to sleep, I pray the Lord my booty to keep,' then think that everything will be all right."

"Miss Eula!" Vincent admonished.

"Well, you can't!"

"If you're speaking from a straight person's point of view, you can't relate, because it's not normal for you," another man named Boris said. "I've been praying and trying to fix it since I was twelve. I know the Lord, but what I feel hasn't changed."

"Then you don't know Jesus," Eula said.

"Miss Eula, you know we don't judge anyone in this group," Vincent warned.

"Okay, fine. But these folks need to stop talking about they were born gay," Eula said firmly. "That is a personal choice. A baby doesn't come in the world saying, 'Waah, waah, I'm gay, Doctor.'"

Several people rolled their eyes at Eula's theatrics, but she didn't seem fazed as she continued. "Lois, tell 'em about your son who prayed for deliverance and was delivered," Eula said to the woman sitting next to her.

"Uh-uh. Don't put me in your mess," Lois said.

Minnie finally spoke up. "God gave us a free will to make choices, and when we make choices that are not pleasing in His sight, He has given us an avenue to make better choices through prayer and repentance." She waved her Bible. "Hallelujah!"

"I was born gay," Boris reiterated, ignoring her. "It was not something I *chose*. I was also born a Christian, and I believe that I was in God's plan, and He makes no mistakes. If it were not His will, I would not exist."

"A lot of things exist that are not God's perfect will— poverty, killing, pedophilia, *Flavor of Love*," Miss Eula snapped. "That doesn't mean it's God's will. It simply means God gives man free will and most of the time y'all just mess it up."

"*Y'all.*" Melvin laughed. "It's judgmental statements like that that keep people who need God away from God! You pass judgment as soon as someone doesn't agree with your standards. That's a great way to win over a soul, lady! I'm sure God is smiling down on you for doing exactly what Jesus would do! *Church folk!*" He shook his head in exasperation.

"Now, now, settle down," Vincent said.

"Well, I think you can pray away the behavior, but if you're really gay, you're always gay," a young woman said, finally speaking up. "I don't know the answer, but I do know that God has done, and continues to do, a great job of judging these things Himself, so He doesn't need any help from us. I'm trying to pray my own horniness away. I figure I'm better off focusing on that."

Jonathan appreciated people's need to talk, but he didn't understand how this was helpful at all. All they were doing was bickering back and forth.

"Can I add my two cents?" Lois asked. "You can't *just* pray anything away. When you are making a change in your life, you have to do more than pray. Your friends change, your ways change, your hangouts change. 'Prayer' and 'faith' are not synonymous. Prayer 'builds up' faith. And that is what gives you the strength to change."

"I believe being truly gay, as opposed to open or curious or something else, is part of your DNA, just like being born with green eyes or red hair," the young woman interjected. "I believe you are born gay or straight, and your actions determine whether you embrace your true sexuality."

"That's foolishness," Minnie said, frustrated with the conversation. "Homosexuality was never a part of God's original plan, and it shall not be a part of His original ending! Leviticus 20:13 says, 'If a man lies with a male as with a woman, both of them have committed an abomination; they shall be put to death, their blood is upon them.'" She defiantly wagged her finger.

Vincent looked like he was getting really irritated. "Don't you believe God created us all? Maybe diversity and sexual orientation is part of that."

"God didn't create Adam and Steve," Eula said emphatically.

"Oh, can you be any more original?" Melvin said, rolling his eyes.

"I'm glad you brought that up," Vincent replied. "I think that verse needs to be placed in context. The authors of the Bible weren't so interested in homosexuality as they were in ensuring a large population. Safety and dominance came in numbers, and their goal was procreation. But keep in mind that same list of verses says you can't have sex with a woman during her period, wear clothes of blended threads and eat shellfish. I don't know about you, but I had shrimp for lunch."

Several people in the room laughed, but Jonathan didn't see anything funny. This had been a complete waste of time. All they'd done was argue and he was still as confused as ever. No, he wouldn't find any answers here. At this rate, Jonathan was beginning to wonder if he'd ever find any answers at all.

Chapter 27

Rachel stood on her toes and peered over the shoulders of the two large men in front of her. She'd hired them specifically for this job. She reckoned that one of the deacons or other church members could control Mary, but she wanted to send a message. And if these six-five, three-hundred-and-fifty-pound linebacker bouncers from the club she used to frequent every Friday night (back before she was a First Lady) couldn't send the message, then no one could.

The two men were positioned at the entrance to Zion Hill. Several members stared strangely at the men as they made their way into Sunday morning service. Rachel had told both men that Mary wouldn't be hard to spot. Zion Hill had only a handful of non-black members, and Mary would be the cocky one carrying a baby. Rachel had no doubt she'd show up at church today. She was probably feeling victorious after Rachel had run off at the park the other day.

They'd been waiting a few minutes when Mary came up the walkway, sashaying like she owned the world, her baby bundled in her arms. Mary also eyed the men strangely but proceeded toward the foyer of the church.

"Excuse me," she said when they stepped in front of her to block her way. "Can I get by?"

"No, ma'am," one of the men said in a deep, guttural voice.

"No? What do you mean, no?" she asked, perplexed.

That was Rachel's cue. She stepped from behind the men. "Just what he said. You're not going in."

"You can't keep me from coming to church," Mary said, looking around like she was expecting someone to come to her aid. Of course, no one did.

"Watch us." Rachel nodded to a man in a cheap gray suit standing a few feet away.

He immediately stepped forward and handed Mary an envelope. "Miss Mary Richardson, you've been served." The man hurried down the stairs before Mary could react.

"Served?" she said. She shifted her baby in her arms, then tore the envelope open. "You're suing me?" she said in disbelief as she read the paper. "Suing me for what?"

"Harassment," Rachel replied. "And I assure you I have more than enough witnesses. But the suit isn't what should concern you. It's the other piece of paper." She pointed to the envelope, and Mary shifted her son to her other arm as she pulled the additional sheet of paper out.

Her mouth dropped open as she read it. "You've taken a restraining order out on me? Are you serious?"

"That's right, a restraining order, barring you from coming anywhere near this church or my home." Rachel crossed her arms with a satisfied smirk. She'd had to pull some major strings to get the restraining order so fast. But thankfully one of her members was a police officer, and he had called in some favors to expedite the process. "The suit will apply only if you violate the order and come anywhere near me or my family."

"I thought you weren't coming back here," Mary spat.

"I said not until you're gone." Rachel pointed to the paper. "And guess what? Poof! You're gone."

"This is crazy." Mary threw the paper to the ground and tried to push past the bodyguards. By now a crowd had gathered on the church grounds. Rachel hated making a spectacle, but it couldn't be avoided.

"Ma'am," one of the men said, grabbing her arm. "I don't want to have to hurt you, 'specially since you got a baby."

Mary stopped, stunned, then said, "Exactly. My baby. *Rev. Adams*'s baby. And my child has a right to see his father!"

"We still don't know if Lester is really his father," Rachel replied.

Mary glanced around at the crowd of people witnessing the standoff. They must have given her a boost of confidence because she raised her voice. "There's no debate, sweetheart. I gave it to the good reverend and I gave it to him good," she said seductively. "And our love affair produced this beautiful baby boy." She held the baby up.

Rachel knew that Mary was trying to get under her skin. *You have the upper hand. Don't let her get to you,* Rachel told herself. "Whatever you think you had with my husband is long over," she calmly replied. "And you are a desperate, pathetic excuse of a woman who probably got knocked up by some john on the street and is trying to pass your baby off as my husband's. What else should I think since you refuse to have a DNA test?"

"I don't need a test!" Mary screamed. The noise caught her son off guard and he jumped. Mary immediately stroked his head to calm him down. She lowered her voice and continued. "You need to face the fact that your husband was in love with me, and he still wants me," she said forcefully.

At that point Lester appeared by his wife's side. Rachel knew that he had remained in the background, trying not to get involved. He didn't agree with the way Rachel was handling this, but right about now he didn't have much say in the matter.

Lester took a deep breath. "Mary, I do not love you. I've never loved you," he declared. "I love my wife." He took in all of the people standing around. "I don't know how many other ways to tell you. I will say it in front of all these people. I made a horrible mistake. I hate that it's had to come to this, but you left us with no other choice. Now please go. And don't come back. You're a distraction here at Zion Hill."

Defeat and embarrassment filled Mary's face. "You're supposed to be a man of God and you're going to put someone out of this church?"

Sister Hicks wobbled over and gently took her arm. "Come on, chile. It's best you go."

Mary snatched her arm away. "Get away from me, old lady."

Sister Hicks immediately raised her cane like she was about to hit Mary. "Ooooh, chile, you better be glad you holding that baby."

Someone rushed to Sister Hicks's side. "No, come on, Miss Ida, she ain't worth it."

"She sure isn't," Rachel said. "And she was just leaving. Or the police will be here in two minutes to arrest her."

Sister Hicks glared at Mary. "The devil ain't welcome here and you ain't nothin' but the devil!" She turned to the woman who had stepped to her side. "Get me inside before I lose my religion."

Mary flung her head back. "Fine, I'm leaving. But you'd better believe, this ain't over," she said. She glared at Lester. "You can't just throw me away."

Her eyes were filling with tears, but Rachel felt no sympathy for her.

"You will regret this, I promise you," Mary growled.

"Ma'am, I'm gonna have to ask you one more time to leave the premises," one of the bouncers said, stepping toward her.

"Leave me alone," she said, pulling away from him as well. "This isn't over, I promise you. This isn't over!" she said again before hoisting her baby up, shoving her way through the crowd and sashaying away.

Chapter 28

A new era had dawned at Zion Hill. Rachel refused to play the victim any longer. Last Sunday she'd shown Mary she meant business, and she'd come to this evening's meeting poised to regain control of her life, at least her public life. Privately, things still weren't so great. Lester was sleeping in the guest room, and she'd decided that until he got a DNA test, he wasn't returning to their bedroom. And if he was never able to get one because his stupid behind had signed the Acknowledgment of Paternity, then well, he just would never come back into the bedroom.

"I need to see some pictures," one of the members named Connie said as they entered the conference room, where they were holding a business meeting. "I didn't go to the picnic, so I need to see her. Did you bring the baby?"

"Nah," Rachel replied. "She has a little cold and I didn't want to bring her out again."

"I hear you, but do you at least have pictures?"

"Of course," Rachel replied, pulling out her baby brag book.

"What's her name?" another member asked as they took their seats.

"Brooklyn."

"Like the bridge?" Sister Hicks asked.

"Yes." Rachel nodded.

Sister Hicks shook her head. "Lord have mercy, if you young-uns ain't naming your kids all this stuff they can't spell till they ten, you giving them those fancy names. Whatever happened to Betty Jean, Barbara Sue?"

Another member named Virginia waved her off. "Don't pay Sister Hicks no never mind. When are you bringing her to church?"

"Oh, probably not until she's older. Outside in the fresh air is one thing, but I'm not quite ready to bring her to church. My stepmom is at the house with her right now."

"Well, we're gonna have to come over and see that precious little baby," Virginia said.

"I am a little surprised to see you at the trustee meeting," Sister Hicks added. These meetings bored Rachel and she usually didn't attend.

"Well, my Good Girlz group have their graduation celebration coming up, and I needed to present to the board and finalize everything for that," she said. "I probably won't stay through the entire meeting. I don't like being away from Brooklyn for long. I'm anxious to get back home."

Connie leaned in. "I don't mean to get all up in your business, but you haven't had any more problems from that Mary girl, have you? I've been praying about it."

Rachel knew Connie well enough to know that she was being genuine. She wasn't the gossipy type. Rachel gently patted her hand. "Thank you for your prayers, Sister Connie. You know we served her with that restraining order last Sunday. And we've had a week with no problems, so, hopefully, she'll finally leave us alone."

Rachel didn't mention that she'd taken Twyla's advice and done some digging for dirt on Mary. She had her friend at the police station checking to see if Mary had a criminal record, anything they could use to bolster their case.

Connie rubbed Rachel's arm in support. "I will definitely keep you in my prayers."

"Thank you," Rachel said. She appreciated the fact that Connie didn't dig for any juicy insider details about Lester's paternity that anyone else would've asked her about.

The trustees began filing into the room. Some of them gave her an uneasy look, but the majority of them smiled sympathetically. Lester came in right behind Deacon Barrett. His eyes met hers. She could tell he wanted to say something, but he merely took his place at the head of the table.

"Hello, church family," Lester began. "I know we have a lot of business to cover, so let's get right to it." He motioned toward Rachel. "Our esteemed First Lady is here to talk about the upcoming project with her mentoring group, the Good Girlz. We'll let her go first because she has to get back home to our precious bundle of joy."

Rachel cleared her throat as Lester sat down.

"Well, I'm very proud to announce that the Good Girlz—" She stopped midsentence as the doors to the conference room swung open. Two men in dingy navy suits walked in like they owned the place. Everyone's attention turned to the pair as they walked to the head of the table. Rachel noticed that two other men, uniformed police officers, were standing in the doorway.

"May we help you?" Lester asked, jumping to his feet.

"Lester Adams?" the taller of the two plainclothesmen asked.

"Yes?"

The man reached in his pocket, pulled out a piece of paper and began reading. "Lester Adams, you are under arrest for the aggravated assault of Mary Richardson." One of the uniformed police officers quickly came over to take Lester's hands and move them behind his back.

"What in the world?" Lester said amid the gasps that reverberated throughout the room.

"You have the right to remain silent. Anything you say can and will be used against you in a court of law."

"What is going on?" Deacon Barrett demanded.

"Sir, I'm going to have to ask you to have a seat," the second plainclothes officer said, flashing a badge.

"You have the right to an attorney," the detective continued as the policeman led Lester toward the door.

Rachel was frozen in place. She had no idea what to do. Lester looked at her. She expected him to protest his innocence, tell the police that there was no way he assaulted that woman. But instead he simply said, "I'm sorry" as they led him out of the room.

Deacon Barrett looked at Rachel like he expected her to follow. When she didn't move, he headed out of the room after the officers. "I'll go find out what's going on," he stated on his way out.

Rachel sat stone-faced. Aggravated assault? Lester was being arrested for *aggravated assault*? No matter what she did, no matter how hard she tried, drama had a way of intruding in her life. But this time her gut was telling her to not sit here and wallow in self-pity. Mary was trying to retaliate. Rachel stood, grabbed her purse, and followed Deacon Barrett out. So this was how Mary was going to make them pay?

"I don't think so," Rachel mumbled. She jumped in her car to follow the police officers downtown. If that trick wanted to do battle, Rachel was ready to wage war.

Chapter 29

A small smile crept over Mary's face as she read the blazing headline on the front page of the *Houston Chronicle.* "Prominent Pastor Arrested for Assaulting Pregnant Mistress."

"I warned you, Lester," Mary mumbled. "I told you I was not playing. You want to sic your barracuda of a wife on me? Bet you wish you had played things my way."

After leaving the church, Mary had immediately gone to the police station with her baby in tow. She'd turned on the waterworks as she'd relayed how Lester had attacked her. She'd told the officer that she'd been scared to come forward initially because she'd been afraid that the next time, Lester would kill her for real. The officer had been sympathetic and had told her they would make "that conniving pastor pay."

Mary had been apprehensive about going to the police—she hated dealing with the cops at all. But this was an extenuating circumstance. Maybe she really couldn't get Lester back, but she dang sure wasn't going to let him and his skank wife win either. Even if the cops eventually dropped all the charges, the bad publicity would cause damage to his reputation and their church.

Mary's vindictive thoughts were interrupted by a loud knock. She walked over to the door. She peeked out to see her neighbor, Mrs. Sloan.

"Hi, Mary. I was taking my walk to the park and wanted to see if you wanted me to take the baby to get some air."

Mary was very appreciative of her neighbor. She couldn't afford a nanny—yet—and Mrs. Sloan gave her the opportunity to have a break. Even though Mary loved her little man to death, she could use a nice long bath and a glass of wine.

"Oh, that would be wonderful," Mary said. "It's about time for him to wake up from his nap anyway. Let me go get him dressed. His stroller is out in the closet on the balcony. You can grab that while I get him ready."

Mary tossed the paper on the coffee table and went to wake up Lester Jr. She was pleasantly surprised to find him awake in his crib, playing with his mobile.

"Such a good baby," Mary said, picking up her son. He smiled at the sight of his mother. "Mommy is sorry you have to live in this dump," she said, sitting him on the worn changing table. "But I promise you things will get better. As soon as your daddy comes to his senses, we'll be living in a big, fancy house like the one he's in now." She knew all about Lester and Rachel's six-thousand-square-foot house. She'd sat outside it many nights, dreaming of the day she'd be able to live like that.

As Mary dressed Lester Jr., she talked about their plans when "his daddy dumped his crazy wife." When Mary returned to the living room, Mrs. Sloan was waiting with the stroller and his diaper bag.

"We're all set," Mrs. Sloan said, tucking his diaper bag underneath the seat. "Oh, that was in his stroller." She held out a package, which was tightly wrapped in brown paper and duct tape.

"It was where?" Mary asked, startled.

"It was tucked down on the side of his stroller. It's wrapped so tightly, I figured it was important." She reached out for the baby. "Come here, little man."

Mary handed the baby over and hesitantly took the package. What in the world could it be? She was trying to figure out how it had gotten in the stroller and why she hadn't seen it when she'd taken the baby out of the stroller yesterday.

Mary walked them to the door, and as soon as they left, she examined the thick package all over. It couldn't be ripped open because it was taped so tightly.

"What is this and where did it come from?" Mary mumbled, going into the kitchen to get a pair of scissors. She cut the package open. Her mouth dropped as a pile of credit cards tumbled out onto the kitchen counter. There had to be a hundred blank credit cards, along with a stack of what looked like payroll checks. She picked up a few of the checks and read. "Joseph Davis, Felix Ruffin, Phillip Williams. What the . . . ?" Each check was made out for twenty-five hundred dollars and drawn on a Delta Airlines commercial account.

"That bastard," she muttered. She knew by now who the package belonged to. She stomped over to the telephone and snatched it up. She punched in Craig's cell phone number. "Craig, have you lost your mind? What is wrong with you?" she screamed as soon as he picked up.

"Whoa, hold on, baby. What's the problem?"

"You're the problem. What in the hell is this you hid in my baby's stroller?" She shook the empty package like he could actually see it.

He chuckled. "I don't know what you're talking about."

"This ain't nobody but you. All these blank credit cards and I know these payroll checks are fake."

"You opened it?" he exclaimed.

"Oh, so now you know what I'm talking about?" She picked up several of the credit cards. "What are you doing with this stuff?"

"I told you I have a plan to make a lot of money."

Mary sighed in frustration. Sometimes, she cursed the day she'd first met Craig. "Where did you get this stuff from? Who did it come from? I'm about to throw this mess away."

A warning buzzed in his voice as he said, "I got it from some people that would be very, very upset if you threw it out."

"Craig, I'm warning you. I don't want to get caught up in any of your madness."

He had the nerve to become aggravated. "Look, just hold the package for another week, all right? I'll get it then."

"No, it's not all right. Come pick up this mess!" Mary exclaimed.

"All right! I'll be by there tomorrow. Just put it up until then. Nosy behind," he snapped.

"I ain't nosy. It's in my home. I can look at it if I want to," she protested.

"Mary, I ain't playing with you! Just leave the stuff alone."

She tried to calm herself down. She couldn't believe he'd stashed illegal merchandise with her. "Craig, I don't know what kind of game you're playing, but I have left that lifestyle behind."

That made him laugh. "Girl, you can't leave it. It's in your blood," he said. "You can't make me believe this whole goin' after the preacher man is because you want to be a preacher's wife. It's a scam, baby. And you'd better chill out before I blow up your spot."

She felt a chill. "What does that mean?"

"Don't get all high society and act like you don't know what I'm talking about," Craig huffed.

"There is nothing to blow up."

He sounded like he was thinking. "Hmmm, let me see, when's the last time we saw each other before recently?"

"Bye, Craig." She didn't even want to go there with him.

"I'm not playing with you, girl. Just put the package up

until I can get to it. I'm branching out on my own, but the people I got this from, they don't play."

"Whatever, Craig. If you don't come get this mess tomorrow, I'm throwing it out!" She slammed the phone down. She couldn't wait to be rid of Craig forever. At this rate, he was sure to mess up her ultimate plan to land Lester.

Chapter 30

If ever Rachel had thought her life couldn't get any worse, she'd definitely been wrong. This had to have been as bad as it got.

"Sweetheart, it could be worse."

Her father was trying his best to find a bright side in this latest development. Rachel clutched the paper tighter and read the headline again. "Prominent Pastor Arrested for Assaulting Pregnant Mistress." Rachel felt her eyes fill with tears. She knew that at one time she hadn't lived her life right, but she'd tried her best to make amends. She'd tried to atone for her past transgressions. So why in the world was she being punished like this?

Jordan and Nia were staying with Jonathan. She'd brought the baby to her father's house expecting a quiet grandfatherly visit while she met with the attorney. But when she saw him ease the newspaper down the side of the sofa, she knew he was hiding something. He had been adamant about not showing her the paper, but she had been just as adamant to see it.

Finally, Simon had let out a long sigh and handed her the paper. Rachel had read the headline in horror. Her heart sank as she read the first two paragraphs. That much alone was enough to make her feel sick to her stomach.

"Daddy, why?"

Brenda lifted the baby out of her seat. "I'll take Brooklyn upstairs and give you two a moment."

Once Brenda walked out of the room, Simon stood and slowly walked to his daughter's side. "I need you to stay calm, okay?"

Rachel forced herself to read the rest of the article. " 'District Attorney Jarvis Johnson is planning to make an example out of what he calls a minister who preys on his congregation.' " Rachel was starting to tremble. "Are they serious?"

"Sweetie, let me have it." He reached for the paper, but Rachel snatched it away and continued reading to the end.

"Did you read this article?" Rachel said, shaking the paper at her father. "This Jarvis Johnson guy is on a mission to—" She stopped and searched for the sentence she was looking for. "—a mission to 'send a message to philandering ministers that you cannot do anything you want to people and expect to get away with it.' " Rachel tossed the paper onto the floor. "He's trying to make an example of Lester."

"Lester is innocent," Simon said. "Anyone who knows him knows that he's not capable of assaulting someone. You said you believe him. Well, I do, too. And I'm confident that justice will prevail."

"Why is this happening to me, Daddy?" Rachel could no longer contain the tears. She'd spent all evening at the jail. Their attorney, Glenn, was working to get Lester out on bail, but so far he wasn't having much luck. "Is God punishing me for everything that I did in the past?"

"Baby girl, God is in the blessing business. He's not in the punishing business."

"What else can explain this? Why else would I have to endure this?"

"Just know that God doesn't give us more than we can bear."

Rachel leaned back onto the sofa and rested her head against the wall. "That's not true," she cried. "Because I can't take any more. This is more than I can handle. This is more than any one person should ever have to bear."

Simon sat down next to his daughter and wrapped his arms around her. He held her as she sobbed into his chest.

"Get it out, baby girl," he said, rocking her back and forth. "I know it's hard, but God can work it all out. I promise you."

"I been tellin' you for years, God don't like ugly."

Rachel and her father looked up in surprise. Minnie was standing in front of them, her hands planted firmly on her hips, a disgusted look on her face.

"Minnie, don't start," Simon began.

"Somebody need to start something," she barked. "This is just the chickens coming home to roost. All the dirt she did,

I don't know how she thought God was gonna give her this happily ever after."

Anger started to overtake Rachel's sadness. She was at her wits' end, and her aunt was about to make her lose it completely.

"Minnie, don't come in here with this mess," Simon warned.

Minnie stomped her foot. "No! I'm family and family tell it like it is. You go doing dirt to people, you gon' get dirt done to you. God is a vengeful God."

Simon jumped to his feet. "Don't you dare go calling what my daughter is going through some retribution from God. Get your own house in order before you come here trying to clean up mine!"

"Somebody needs to do it," she fired back. "Because you always been too weak to keep your family under control."

Rachel had never seen such fury light her father's eyes. He slowly rocked back and forth, like he was trying to calm himself down. Silence filled the room before Simon softly said, "Do your sons know about their other siblings?"

Minnie's eyes grew wide. "What other siblings?"

"Don't play dumb, Minnie. Otis's other family." He glared at her. "You know, the one you think nobody knows about. The reason you had that poor man cremated instead of giving him a funeral so that his other wife and kids wouldn't show up."

Minnie looked horrified.

"Do you think people didn't know that? I know it, just like I know Otis hated being married to you, and I can't say that I blame him. Just like I believe you had something to do with his death. Word around the family is you poisoned the man. I don't know if it's true, but his sudden death was mighty suspicious."

"How dare you—"

"How dare I what? Throw it in your face? I haven't all these years. I let you live in your fantasy world. I let you throw rocks when you were living in a glass house yourself. But you've pushed me too far!"

Rachel was stunned. Her tears had dried up as she'd watched the exchange between her father and aunt. Aunt Minnie had all that going on?

"Simon, how could you . . ." Minnie's voice took on a deflated tone that Rachel had never heard.

"No, Minnie, I'm sorry, but somebody needs to put you in your place. You already were a mess to deal with, but Otis's betrayal made you unbearable. You are a bitter old woman who failed in her marriage, with her kids and with her life, and now you are trying to seek refuge in the Word. Only you're twisting the Word to fit what you want. You stand in judgment of everybody, and enough is enough!"

Minnie fixed her brother with a look of hatred. The longer she stared, the more her resolve seemed to be strengthening. "So, I come here trying to help this harlot of a daughter you have," she spat, tossing her hand Rachel's way, "and you want to turn this around on me?"

Simon was about to reply when Rachel stood up. "Aunt Minnie, you don't know anything about me," she said, "or what's going on in my household."

Minnie pointed to the newspaper. "I know your bed-jumpin' husband got somebody else pregnant, then tried to assault her and is now behind bars. I know that much. And he wanna call himself a man of God."

Simon stepped forward, but Rachel put a hand on his chest to stop him. She would handle her own business. "At least Lester didn't despise me so much that he ran off and married someone else." That shut Minnie up, and Rachel continued, "I know my husband made a mistake, everybody knows it. But I also know he ain't put his hands on nobody. He is a man of God, but he's still just a man. Who still falls short. So I'm not gonna let you sit here and talk about him like a dog." Rachel was surprising herself by what she was saying, but watching her aunt—the bitterness, the judgmental words—she knew that she wouldn't allow herself to end up like that.

"You just a bed-hopping whore and so is your husband," Minnie said.

"Then I guess it runs in the family, because it sounds like Uncle Otis was the biggest whore of all," Rachel hissed.

Minnie reached out and slapped Rachel dead across the cheek. Stunned, Rachel instinctively slapped her aunt right back.

Minnie gasped as she grabbed her cheek. "Oh, my Lord. Simon, are you gonna let this gal put her hands on me?"

Simon looked stunned himself, but he quickly recovered. "I'd say you had that one coming," he finally said. "And if she didn't do it, I probably would have done it myself."

"Well, I'm not gonna stand here and take this!" Minnie

turned and stomped out of the den. She mumbled a string of curse words as she exited. So much for her religion.

Both Rachel and her father exhaled as Minnie walked away. Simon turned to his daughter and smiled.

"Dad, I'm so sorry for being disrespectful, but you know I was on the edge and she just jumped all over me," Rachel said.

Simon chuckled. "Please, she had that coming. Somebody probably should've slapped her mouth shut a long time ago."

"You know you're going to hear about that later." Rachel shook her head in exasperation.

Simon flicked his hand. "I'm not studying Minnie. But I am proud of you."

"Me?" That's the last thing she expected to hear from her father. At one time, she'd barely gotten his attention, let alone his praise. But after Loretta had died, their relationship had improved dramatically. "What would you be proud of me for?"

"Proud of you for fighting for your man."

Rachel allowed a smile as she lowered her head. "I didn't know I had any fight left."

Simon gently lifted her chin. "You do. You know something? The devil is hard at work, and you're going to need every ounce of fight to make it through this. But if anybody can do it, you can."

Rachel weighed her father's words. For the first time since Mary had come crashing into their lives, she actually believed she could fight her way through this.

Chapter 31

Jonathan was leaning over the secretary's desk, laughing as she recounted her blind date, when the office door swung open with unimaginable force. All eyes turned to the man towering in the doorway. Mr. Hurst looked like a raging bull.

"You!" he yelled, spotting Jonathan. "This is all your fault!"

He charged toward Jonathan, who was able to jump out of the way.

"Mr. Hurst!" Jonathan said, ducking behind one of the office desks. "What in the world is wrong with you?"

"You! You are what's wrong with me. I told you to stay away from my son!"

Jonathan noticed he was holding a large canvas in his hand. It was some type of drawing. "You teaching my son all this homo stuff!" Mr. Hurst violently shook the canvas at Jonathan.

"What in God's name is going on out here?"

Jonathan was relieved to see his boss, the school principal, Tim Albert.

"Get me the person in charge!" Mr. Hurst screamed.

The entire office was at a standstill as everyone watched the unfolding scene.

"I'm the principal," Mr. Albert said. "And before anything happens, I'm going to ask you to calm down or I will have you thrown off the premises."

Mr. Hurst jabbed his finger in Jonathan's direction. "You need to have that fa—"

"Mr. Hurst!" Mr. Albert said, cutting him off. "May I remind you that we have students here. I will not allow you to come in here acting a fool."

Mr. Hurst glared at Jonathan, his nostrils flaring, but he did settle down.

"Now, will you please step in my office and tell me what's going on?" Mr. Albert turned to Jonathan. "You too, Mr. Jackson." He glanced around at the few students, teachers and office workers that were frozen, too scared to move. "Everyone else, back to work and your classrooms. The show is over!" He headed back into his office.

Jonathan waited for Mr. Hurst to follow before he moved an inch. Mr. Hurst stomped into the office like a man on a mission. "Call security," Jonathan mumbled to the secretary before heading into the office himself.

Inside the office, Mr. Albert took a seat at his desk, then motioned for Mr. Hurst to sit as well. He declined.

"Do you want to tell me what this is about?" Mr. Albert said.

"It's about this." Mr. Hurst slammed the canvas onto the desk.

Jonathan's jaw dropped open at the drawing of a nude Benjamin Morris.

"My son drew that." Mr. Hurst stabbed the painting with a meaty finger. "Apparently it's that queer boy that goes here. He posed for it!" Mr. Hurst said, like it was the most disgusting thing he'd ever seen.

Mr. Albert picked the canvas up and studied it, his face remaining expressionless. Jonathan, meanwhile, was dumbfounded. He'd had no clue Roderick had been intending to draw a male nude.

"Why did Roderick draw this?" Mr. Albert asked.

"Ask funny man over here," Mr. Hurst said, jabbing the air toward Jonathan.

"Mr. Jackson, do you know what this is all about?"

Jonathan slowly shook his head. "I have no idea."

"Roderick said it was part of the admissions packet you gave him for art school," Mr. Hurst snapped. "You may get your rocks off by seeing naked men, but how dare you try to push that perversion off on my son?"

"Mr. Hurst, I assure you, at no time did I ever tell Roderick to draw anyone, let alone anyone without their clothes on," Jonathan said.

"What did you tell him?" Mr. Albert asked.

"I just gave him the admissions information for several art schools," Jonathan protested. "That's it."

"Ain't no son of mine going to art school!" Mr. Hurst bellowed. "And I thought I told you to stay away from him?"

Jonathan ignored the outburst as he continued. "I know one of the applications said he needed to submit some observational art, which can be a human model. He said he didn't have anything, but he could draw something. But at no time did he say anything about what he was drawing. Mr. Albert, you know I would never encourage that."

Mr. Albert loudly exhaled as he set the picture down. "Mr. Hurst, I assure you, Mr. Jackson is one of our most highly regarded counselors."

"I don't care if he was hired by Jesus himself. I don't want him anywhere near my son!"

"Mr. Hurst, that really isn't—"

He slammed his palm down on the desk. "Did you hear what I said!"

Mr. Albert stood, eye to eye, and calmly yet sternly said, "Mr. Hurst, I will not be intimidated or threatened."

"It ain't a threat, it's a promise. Keep that homo away from my son or there'll be hell to pay." With that, Mr. Hurst spun around and marched out of the office.

"What just happened?" a stunned Jonathan asked after the door slammed closed.

Mr. Albert sighed heavily and sank back into his seat. "Yet another unruly and unrealistic parent." He leaned forward and studied the drawing again. "You sure you didn't know anything about this?"

"Absolutely, Mr. Albert," Jonathan replied. "There is no

way I would condone, let alone encourage, something like this."

"Is this who I think it is?" Mr. Albert asked.

Jonathan nodded. There was no doubt that was Benjamin. Roderick was definitely talented at drawing.

"That Morris boy has been nothing but trouble." Mr. Albert scratched his head. "Do you think something is, ah . . ."

Jonathan knew where he was going. "Honestly, I don't know. I don't think Roderick even knows. But as he is a confused young man trying to find his way, I do know that Benjamin is not the type of person he needs to be around." Jonathan suddenly felt a pang of guilt. If he felt that way, why couldn't he have just come right out and said something to Roderick? *Because you didn't want to appear biased,* the voice in his head said.

"Well, look, just to avoid any drama, let's have Mrs. Balaski handle Roderick from now on." Mr. Albert picked up the drawing and set it on the side of his desk. "It's obvious his caveman father isn't someone to reason with, so just to avoid any issues, we'll handle it like that."

Jonathan thought about protesting. He felt like no one could understand Roderick like he could. But he knew Mr. Albert was right. Staying out of Roderick's life was best for everyone.

Chapter 32

If someone had ever told Rachel Jackson Adams that she would one day be sitting on the other side of a window at the Harris County jail, visiting her incarcerated husband, who was behind bars for assaulting his mistress, she would've told them they were crazy. But lo and behold, here she was.

She took her measure of her husband through the grainy glass. After twenty-six long hours, she'd finally been able to return. Each minute that had passed had made her more and more angry that she was in this humiliating position.

Lester motioned toward the phone again. "Please pick up the phone," he mouthed.

She took a deep breath and picked up the phone.

"Thank you for coming," he said.

Rachel just held the phone by her ear. What could she say?

Yes, Lester had told her about the accident, but he hadn't mentioned anything about an assault.

"I need you to know that I'm not guilty," Lester began.

"I saw the pictures, Lester," Rachel informed him tersely. She'd spoken to her friend, Lydia Simmons, a longtime member of Zion Hill, less than an hour ago. Lydia wasn't supposed to, but she'd shown Rachel some of the evidence against Lester. Mary might have been playing dirty, but the photos didn't lie. "I saw what you did. The bruises. The stitches. The police say you did that."

"Rachel, you know I'm not capable of something like that."

She did, but that still didn't explain the pictures. "It seems like I don't know what you're capable of anymore."

Lester massaged his temples. "I didn't hurt her. I mean, it was an accident."

"Which is it, Lester? Did you do it or didn't you?"

"It's not like that at all," he protested.

"Then what is it like, Lester? Please explain it to me, because I'm having a real hard time understanding."

He seemed resigned to her contempt. "Rachel, the night Mary went into labor I went to talk with her—"

"Yeah, you told me all of that, but somehow you left out the assault part. Just like you left out the fact that you signed that Acknowledgment of Paternity. Omission is just as bad as lying, Lester."

"Well, the reason she went into labor . . . was b-because she came on to me and I pushed her away. That's when she fell."

Rachel studied him carefully. He'd become such a good liar

that she didn't know what to believe anymore. "The bruises on her arms?"

"The bruises came from when I squeezed her to try to push her away. I guess she bruises easily. I swear to you, I wasn't trying to hurt her. I was just trying to get her off me. She stumbled and lost her balance, and that's how she fell on the table. The glass broke and cut her. It almost killed the baby. I was so scared. It's why I went to the hospital." He lowered his head in shame. "It's why I signed the Acknowledgment of Paternity. She threatened to go to the cops and file assault charges."

"Well, it looks like she went anyway."

Lester was in despair. "Rachel, you know I wouldn't hurt anyone."

That rang true. Lester might have been a liar and a cheater, but he definitely wasn't an abuser. Okay, she could accept that explanation. Mary had twisted the facts to suit her own purposes. Rachel needed to move past that and figure out what their next move would be.

"So now what?" she asked.

"Please tell me you believe me," he said.

She couldn't do that. She couldn't make him think everything was fine.

"Lester, right now you need to focus on getting out of here. I talked to Glenn and your case doesn't look good," she said, referring to their attorney.

"What does that mean?"

"It means you're in a whole lot of trouble. The good thing is, Glenn says you'll probably get bail. He's working on that now." She tapped the glass, then pointed at herself. "But don't worry, I'm going to handle it from here. I tried to let you handle this and look what happened. Now we do things my way." Rachel stood up, ready to go.

"Are you leaving?"

"I have to go handle this. I'll talk to you soon." Rachel didn't give him time to reply as she turned and headed out. She'd barely gotten out of the building when she picked up the phone to call Lydia, who was trying to dig up dirt on Mary.

"Hey, Lydia," Rachel said after Lydia answered her cell. "I was just checking in to see if you'd had any luck."

"Hi, Rachel," Lydia replied. "Give me a minute." Rachel heard shuffling, some voices in the background, then a blank lull of silence. "Sorry, I had to step in the bathroom." Lydia let out a heavy sigh. "I'm sorry, I haven't had any luck."

"So she's not in your system?" Rachel asked. She felt deflated, for she was almost sure Mary had a record or something that they could use to their advantage.

"That's just it," Lydia said, puzzlement in her voice. "There's nothing on her period. Not even a driver's license."

"What?"

"Yeah. You know what I'm thinking? If she's as shady as you say she is, maybe she's operating under an alias. Do you have a photo of her? I could run her through our system that way."

Rachel thought long and hard. Where in the world would she get a photo? Her eyes lit up when she remembered their new member orientation process. They always took a picture of the new members, and she was sure they had one from when Mary had joined two years ago.

"Lydia, give me till tomorrow. I know how I can get a photo."

"Great. Then we can know for sure what this Mary Richardson is hiding."

Rachel thanked her friend and paused as she contemplated her next move. She couldn't go home and wait—for Lydia or Lester. No, if she was taking matters into her own hands, she would have to push the envelope, and she knew exactly what that meant her next move would be.

Chapter 33

"Knock, knock."

Jonathan tensed up at the sight of Roderick sticking his head through his office door.

"Hi, Roderick, how may I help you?" He didn't mean to sound cold, but Mr. Hurst's outburst the other day was fresh in his mind, and the last thing he wanted was more drama.

Roderick took the greeting as his cue to enter. "I'm sorry to disturb you, but I was wondering if I could talk to you."

It hurt Jonathan's heart to see the look of distress on Roderick's face, but still, he said, "I'm a little busy right now."

Roderick looked shocked. "But you said your door was always open."

Jonathan set his pen down and intertwined his fingers. He needed to weigh his words carefully. "I meant that, but I've been doing some thinking, and I think Mrs. Balaski would be better at helping you with any issue you may have."

A stunned expression crossed the boy's face. "But I don't wanna talk to Mrs. Balaski. I wanna talk to you."

"I understand that, Roderick, but—"

"Is this about my dad coming here? Everyone was talking about it," he said frantically. " 'Cause if that's what it's about, I'm sorry about that. I hid my drawing, but he found it. And I know I told him you gave me the applications, but I told him you didn't know nothing about the drawing. I swear."

Jonathan put his palms face out, trying to calm Roderick down. He wanted to ask him about the drawing, get to the bottom of why he'd done it, but Mr. Albert had been very clear. Jonathan needed to send Roderick to the other counselor. "I understand that, but your father thinks it's best if you deal with Mrs. Balaski."

"My father doesn't know anything about me!" Roderick yelled. "He doesn't try to understand me. You're the only one who does. You're the only one I feel comfortable talking to."

"I understand that, Roderick. But—"

"But you're turning your back on me like everybody else!" Roderick snapped.

"Now, you know that's not true."

"Yes, it is!" he cried. "Everybody at school is talking about what happened. I'm just glad Rodney is away visiting that college in Nebraska or he would be in all kinds of fights. Trent and his boys didn't even see the drawing and they've been riding me all day! And Benjamin is acting like it's no big deal."

Say Amen, Again

Jonathan wanted so bad to sit Roderick down and convince him to stay as far away from Benjamin as possible. Instead he said blandly, "All issues Mrs. Balaski should be able to help you with."

Roderick's eyes were filming with tears. "You know what, I don't need nobody to help me with nothing." He took the manila folder that he had clutched in his hand, flung it across the floor, then stormed out of the office.

Chapter 34

"So, do you think he's going to be a problem?" Bernice leaned back on Mary's all-white sofa as Mary paced back and forth across the living room. Mary had been stressed out since finding Craig's package. Two days later, he still hadn't shown up to get it. Mary didn't want any trouble, and that package was nothing but trouble. Craig was up to his old tricks and she didn't want to get sucked in.

"Yes, without a doubt he's gonna be a problem," Mary lamented. "He thinks I'm running some type of scam and he wants in."

The look on Bernice's face made Mary stop in her tracks.

"What?" Mary asked.

"Well, are you?" Bernice finally asked.

"I don't believe you," Mary said. "No, I'm not. I genuinely love Lester."

"I mean, how? It's not like you guys were together for long or anything," Bernice said doubtfully.

"How long were you with Tommy before you fell in love?"

Bernice looked like she was thinking. "A week and a half."

"I rest my case."

"But you see how that turned out." Tommy was Bernice's last boyfriend. He'd turned out to be a bigamist who was wanted in two different states.

"That's not the point," Mary protested.

"What is the point?" Bernice crossed her legs to get comfortable. She and Mary had been friends only for the last year, but they were like two peas in a pod. Since Bernice was always looking for a way to come up, Mary could understand why she would think that's all this was to Mary as well.

"If I can get Lester to see that I'm the one he was meant to be with, he'll come around—and be a father to my baby and a husband to me," Mary explained.

Bernice shook her head like she wasn't convinced. "If you say so."

"I say so." Mary sighed. "Look, let's just change the subject. I haven't told you yet, but I got a job interview."

Bernice's eyes widened. "What? You working?"

"I don't have much choice. My money is running real low, and until Lester's child support kicks in, I'm stuck."

"Have you filed on him?"

"I sure have."

"But don't you need a DNA test?"

"Not when you have an Acknowledgment of Paternity, and I do."

Bernice smiled as she high-fived Mary. "I wanna be like you when I grow up. Now, tell me about this job."

"It's crazy. It came out of nowhere. It's working in the front office of the Houston Rockets."

"Girl, shut yo' mouth!" Bernice exclaimed. "Why didn't you tell me you were trying to get a job there? I'd love to work there so I could meet me a pro baller."

"I know, right? I didn't apply there directly, though. They said they got my résumé from some online site where I had posted it. I don't even remember which one."

"Well, dang. That's what I'm talking about. Good luck, because if things don't work out with the pastor, you're right in the mix of things to snag you another man. A rich man at that."

Mary smiled, because she wouldn't need any pro ballers. When all was said and done, she was confident that she'd snag her man.

Chapter 35

It had taken some maneuvering, but Rachel had managed to get what she needed. She'd gone by the church early this morning and lifted a photo of Mary out of the church files. She'd take it over to Lydia at the police station—after she handled her second order of business.

Rachel pushed her sunglasses up on her face and scooted closer to the woman holding the baby.

"He's a handsome little fella, isn't he?" Rachel said.

"He sure is," the woman replied.

Rachel leaned over and smiled at the baby. She studied his face for any signs of Lester. There were none. But she couldn't tell if that was because she wanted so bad not to see any, or if there really was no resemblance.

She tickled the baby's cheek, noting his head full of curly hair. *Just what she needed.*

"Is that your child?" Rachel asked.

"Heavens no." The woman laughed. "Do I look young enough to have a baby?" She smiled warmly. "This is my neighbor's son. I just watch him from time to time to give her a break. She's a good mom. She loves this baby so much. But even the best of moms need a break sometimes."

Rachel tried to stifle her frown. She wanted to hear that Mary was a horrible mother, not deserving of a child.

"Can I hold him?" Rachel asked.

"Oh, I don't know about that," the woman said nervously.

"Oh, I'll just sit right here. That's my daughter playing over on the slide." Rachel pointed to a random little girl nearby. "I just love babies," Rachel said as the woman looked on hesitantly. "I just had one myself, but she's at home with her dad so I could spend some quality time with my daughter."

"That's so sweet," the woman said. She looked down at the baby. "Well, I guess it won't do any harm for you to hold him. But I will have to ask you to sanitize your hands."

Rachel chuckled. "That's not a problem. In fact"—she reached into her purse and pulled out a bottle of hand sanitizer spray—"I'm all on it." She sprayed both of her hands, then rubbed them together before reaching out for the baby. He was absolutely adorable. Too bad his mom was an evil witch.

The woman watched with an eagle eye as Rachel bounced the baby. As the baby giggled, Rachel took the blue blanket and began playing peekaboo. She covered his face, then pulled it away. The baby didn't seem to be fazed, but on the third time, Rachel eased her hand behind his head and silently muttered a quick apology, then yanked as hard as she could. The baby let out a piercing scream.

"Oh, no, what's wrong?" the woman said.

"I don't know," Rachel said. "He just started yelling."

"Oooh, no, don't cry," the woman said, taking him away from Rachel. He was screaming at the top of his lungs.

"I'm sorry, I don't know what happened. Maybe the peekaboo game scared him," Rachel said. She felt awful, but she couldn't have broken out the scissors that were in her purse, since the woman was watching her so closely.

The woman began bouncing the baby, trying to calm him down. Rachel glanced down at her hand. She'd managed to get three hairs. She said a silent prayer for God to forgive her for hurting the baby, but it had been the only way. She pulled out a Kleenex and eased the hair into it.

"I'm sorry, I'll let you get back to tending to him," Rachel said.

She hurried off, trying her best to contain her smile. *Yeah, Mary, so much for your agreeing to a DNA test,* Rachel mumbled. She didn't need Mary's cooperation, after all. God had worked it all out.

"Somehow, I don't think God planned for you to steal hair from a baby to get to the bottom of its paternity," Twyla said, shaking her head in disbelief.

Rachel had gone straight to Twyla's with the hair sample, since Twyla's aunt ran a DNA testing business.

ReShonda Tate Billingsley

"Why do you think I had you call Mary in for a job interview?" Rachel asked.

"I didn't know. You wouldn't tell me, remember?" Twyla said. "And how did you know she was leaving the baby with the neighbor and that the neighbor would take the baby to the park?"

Rachel smiled mischievously. "I made Lester call and say he wanted to bring some money by today when I knew she'd be out for the interview. She told him she was leaving the baby with her neighbor while she was out and told him to come later. Of course, he's not coming."

"Does Lester know what you were doing?"

She shook her head with a big smile. "All I told him was I had a plan. He's the one who created this mess, so he knew he needed to let me do my thing." Rachel was proud of how everything had fallen into place. "I was all prepared to go knock on that woman's door and tell her I was a relative or something when I saw her leave for the park with the baby, so I followed them."

Twyla laughed. "The old Rachel is back! Man, I would've given anything to see the look on Mary's face when she got to the Houston Rockets' head office and found out there was no interview."

"Well, I had you do that so I could get this." Rachel held up the hair, which she'd placed in a small plastic bag. "What did you think I had planned?"

"I don't know. I thought you were going to break into her

house or something," Twyla said. "I didn't think you'd stalk her sitter, then steal her baby's hair. And did you have to yank it? You couldn't just comb it or something?"

"I didn't have time for all that," Rachel said, frowning at the memory. "I told the baby I was sorry."

"Oh, okay, then, that makes it better."

"Look, you're the one who told me to fight back. That's what I'm doing."

"If you say so." Twyla shrugged. "So now what?"

"So now you call your aunt down at the DNA lab and tell her to get to work." Rachel removed another plastic bag. "I went home and got some hair out of Lester's hairbrush."

Twyla was impressed with her friend's sleuthing. "You're lucky Lester has hair. I'd be in trouble if it was Tony. He's been bald for so many years, I'd have to try to pluck some of the hair from his chest," Twyla joked.

"Can you stay focused here?"

"Okay, fine. I'll call her tomorrow."

"Look," Rachel said, standing to leave, "this woman is trying to destroy my family and I'm not having it. I need you to stress to your aunt that I need this info asap."

"Fine, and may I say that although I don't approve of your methods, I am happy to see you're fighting back and not just sitting back and torturing Lester."

"Oh, Lester is not out of the woods yet. If these results"— she waved the bag—"come back and prove, as Mary says, that he is the father . . ." Rachel's words trailed off. She wasn't ready to say that she would leave, but she knew that's what would happen. She couldn't stay. She couldn't have a lifetime of Mary's interference. "I . . . I don't know what I'll do, Twyla." Her voice choked up.

Twyla rushed over to hug her friend. "Let's cross that bridge when you get to it," Twyla said comfortingly. "You're right, Mary is a low-down dirty skank, and I will say it again, I don't believe this baby is Lester's."

Rachel pulled back and smiled. "You don't sound very convinced."

"I don't?"

Rachel cut her eyes at Twyla. "Okay, I'm not," Twyla admitted. "But we don't need all that negativity. Give me the bags and I'll call my aunt and see if she can put a rush on it."

"Thank you, Twyla. You're a lifesaver."

Twyla held up the Baggies. "I hope the results can be a marriage saver." She gave Rachel a speculative look. "No matter which way they come out, you can make it through this."

"Twyla, I'm trying not to go there."

"Okay, I'm just saying," Twyla said. "I'll let you know what my aunt says."

Rachel stood and hugged her friend.

"Are you about to go home?" Twyla asked.

Rachel shook her head. "Nope, heading down to the station to see Lydia and give her Mary's photo. See what we can dig up there."

Twyla smiled slyly and waggled her finger at Rachel.

"What?" Rachel said, heading toward the door. "You said I needed to fight back."

"Well, go on, Muhammad Ali," Twyla said as she followed her. "My friend is back and with a vengeance. That's what I'm talking about."

Rachel laughed as she made her way back to her car, praying that her faith and efforts would yield positive results.

Chapter 36

It had taken Rachel almost forty-five minutes to get to the police station because of an accident on Highway 59. But she was finally sitting in a conference room at the police station, waiting for Lydia.

"Hey, Rachel, sorry to keep you waiting," Lydia said as she marched into the room. "It's been kinda hectic around here."

"No problem."

"So, whatcha got?" Lydia said, sliding into the seat across the table.

Rachel took the photo out of her purse and pushed it across to Lydia. "This is Mary Richardson."

"What a convenient name," Lydia said as she picked up the photo and examined it.

"So you really think she might be using an alias?"

Lydia shrugged. "You never know. Especially since she's not in the system at all, not even a parking ticket. Something doesn't smell right about that."

"Well, how will her photo help?"

"I can run it through our database and see if it matches anything. If so, we might be able to see if she's using an alias or if she's got a record." Lydia eyed Rachel. "But what do you plan to do with the information?"

Rachel blew out a frustrated breath. "She has accused Lester of assault. I'm trying to gather any information I can on her. It's like she appeared out of nowhere, and I'm trying to see what dirt I can find on her to help our case."

"Speaking of the case, how's that going? George told me Lester made bail," she said, referring to her husband and Lester's childhood friend.

Rachel let out a long sigh and Lydia squeezed her hand. "I'm trying to stay strong, but I realized as hard as it is for me, it's twice as hard for Lester." Rachel couldn't believe she was saying that, but the weariness in her husband's eyes when she'd picked him up after his release from jail yesterday had tugged at her heart. Despite the fact that they were in this position because of his actions, she couldn't help but feel a tinge of sympathy. "Can you believe the district attorney had the nerve to offer Lester a plea deal?"

"Of course I can," Lydia said, a cynic about the court system. "That's how they operate. But if he's innocent, tell him don't take it. The last thing he needs to do is get in the system."

"He's innocent, and don't worry, Lester isn't pleading to anything."

Lydia stood up, glad to hear it. "Good. I know Rev. Adams, and this case stinks to high heaven."

"Lydia, you don't know how much this means to me," Rachel said as she stood as well. "This woman has made my life a living hell and we've got to stop her."

"Well, I don't know what I'll turn up, but I'll definitely try. I'll let you know something tomorrow."

Chapter 37

"Hey, you two need to cut all of that out," Jonathan said as he broke up a young boy and girl kissing near the back stairwell of the school building.

"Sorry, Mr. Jackson," the girl giggled.

He motioned toward her shirt. "Fix yourself up."

She looked down at her bra, which had been unfastened and was sitting lopsided on her chest. She giggled again. The boy bore a boastful expression. Jonathan shook his head. The fact that the girl was fourteen and didn't see anything wrong with being felt up in public was pretty sad.

"Miss Conyers, I'd like to see you in my office before the end of the day, please?" Jonathan said.

"What? What did I do?" she said, suddenly losing her smile.

"Either come talk to me, or you can go talk to the principal.

Matter of fact, I'd like to talk to both of you. Come see me during lunch period."

They groaned and stomped off. Jonathan made his way toward his office. He'd just opened the door when he heard the sound of a gunshot. Everyone in the front office immediately turned in the direction where the shot rang out. Instinctively, Jonathan took off outside.

As he reached the outside door, he heard several screams. Jonathan and another administrator rounded the corner at the same time and noticed the body on the ground, a pool of blood forming beneath it.

A young man named Trent, who was known around campus as the school bully, stood over the body. Trent looked like he was in shock as splatters of blood covered his face.

Jonathan was about to ask what happened when he noticed who was lying on the ground. Roderick Hurst.

"What happened?" another teacher asked as Jonathan fell to his knees and grabbed Roderick's hand.

"Someone call 9-1-1!" Jonathan cried, feeling for a pulse.

Trent didn't reply as he stared wide-eyed, his mouth open.

"I already did, Mr. Jackson," some student yelled from the small crowd that was gathering.

"Roderick! Roderick!" Jonathan said, gently shaking him. Roderick's eyes were closed. A small bullet hole had opened the side of his head. Jonathan felt like he was going to be sick.

"What happened?" one of the assistant principals asked as he arrived on the scene.

Trent still didn't say anything, but another boy standing

next to him said, "He—he just shot himself. Right here in front of everybody."

By that point, more teachers and campus security had arrived. More screams and cries spread throughout the crowd.

"Get back, get back," a security officer said as the wail of sirens echoed in the background.

Jonathan continued searching Roderick's wrist for a pulse. He couldn't feel anything, but then again, Jonathan's heart was beating so fast that he didn't know if he was even taking the pulse the right way.

The school nurse finally appeared. "Let me see," she said, pushing Jonathan out of the way. She knelt down, checked his pulse, leaned in and listened for his breath. A sick feeling engulfed Jonathan as she glanced up at him. The look in her eyes told Jonathan what he already knew—Roderick was dead.

Just then Rodney came barreling around the corner. He stopped abruptly when he saw his brother lying on the ground. "Rod-Roderick!" he cried as he fell to the ground. "Man, wake up! Wake up!" Rodney was hysterical as he shook his brother.

The entire scene was chaotic and heartbreaking. Two teachers tried to go to Rodney's side. "Come on, son, he's gone," one of the teachers said.

"No, no, no!" Rodney wailed. He fought them off as he screamed and cried as he pulled his brother's head into his lap. "Roderick, no, no, no!" he cried as he rocked back and forth. "Who did this to you?"

The boy who had spoken up a minute ago was now tight-lipped. Then Jonathan noticed the gun lying next to Roderick's body. The principal, Mr. Albert, spotted it at the same time.

"Whose is this?" Mr. Albert asked, using a handkerchief to pick it up. "Who does this belong to?"

"It's his," another boy said, pointing to Roderick. "He really did shoot himself."

"Security, get these kids out of here!" Mr. Albert demanded. "Someone help get Rodney out of here." He turned to Jonathan. "Mr. Jackson, bring these boys to my office now!" He pointed to Trent and the two boys standing next to him.

Trent didn't move, and Jonathan had to nudge him. "Let's go," Jonathan said. He shuttled the boys into the principal's office. Trent—all six feet of him—was in tears. The other two boys were in shock as well.

"Okay, does someone want to tell me what happened?" Mr. Albert asked as he entered the office. Two campus police officers were with him. He slammed his door shut and stood with his arms crossed. "And this is not the time for lies. I need somebody to tell me what is going on."

"We-we were just messing with him," Trent said quietly. "Just teasing him and stuff and next thing we knew, he pulled a gun on us."

"A *gun*?" Jonathan said. "Where would Roderick get a gun?" The pain in his gut deepened. Is that what Roderick had wanted to talk to him about? Had it reached that point of retaliation? Jonathan would never know, because he'd basically turned his back on Roderick. He struggled to contain his feelings.

"Man, I don't know," Trent cried. "It just came out of

nowhere. He grabbed it out of his backpack and pulled it on us. I thought he was going to shoot us. And he was just waving it at us and pointing it and telling us he was fed up and now we were gonna be sorry."

"Sorry for what?" Jonathan couldn't help asking.

Trent shrugged as he tried to fight back tears. "Messin' with him all the time, I guess. I don't know. All I know is he had the gun pointed at us, he was crying, then he turned the gun on himself. He shot himself right there in front of us," Trent said, like he was still trying to believe the shooting had actually happened.

Jonathan fell silent. He should've recognized that Roderick was capable of something like this. *Why* hadn't he recognized that the situation had gotten that bad? *Because you turned your back on him,* a little voice in his head said.

Their conversation was interrupted by a commotion from the hallway. Jonathan glanced out the door. Another counselor, two teachers and a security officer were still trying to calm down an anguished Rodney. Jonathan wanted to cry himself. He'd failed both of the twins. He was supposed to be a counselor and he'd allowed his own personal issues to get in the way of his job. And now a young man had paid the ultimate price. Jonathan didn't know how he'd ever forgive himself.

Chapter 38

Rachel had never been so relieved to see someone. Twyla had really worked her magic. Not even twenty-four hours had passed and here she was, back with the results. Rachel, Twyla and Lester were gathered in the living room. Lester had just come in from the gym. He could tell they were up to something because he looked back and forth between the two of them.

"What's going on?"

Rachel hadn't figured out how she was going to break the news. All she knew was they finally were about to find out if Lester was the father of Mary's baby. Hopefully, this piece of paper would be enough to stop Mary.

"It's no sense in holding out," Rachel conceded. "Lester, we did a DNA test on Mary's baby."

"What? How?" Lester asked, astonished. "Is this why you had me call her?"

"Don't worry about that," Rachel replied. "You couldn't get it done, so I had to take matters into my own hands."

Lester wanted to protest, but he knew better than to push the issue any further. So he dropped his duffel bag and nervously bit down on his bottom lip.

"Well?" he asked.

"Do you guys want me to give you privacy?" Twyla said. Rachel knew that Twyla wanted to know just as bad, and since she already knew all of their dirt, she might as well stay. Plus, Rachel might need Twyla to be there to keep her from losing it if these results came back positive.

"You're good." Rachel fingered the envelope. "I just want to know."

"D-do you mind if I sit down?" Lester stammered.

Rachel glared at him as he eased down on the sofa. She took a deep breath, then flipped the envelope over. The house was eerily silent as they all waited for her to rip the envelope open. Rachel closed her eyes and inhaled again.

Dear God, I know I've done a lot of stuff in my life, but please, please don't let this be Lester's child, she prayed.

She opened her eyes to see Lester with his head bowed and his eyes squeezed tightly as well. He was praying, too. Rachel inhaled again, then pulled the paper out of the envelope and read the results.

Based on testing results, the probability that Lester Adams is the father of Baby Boy Adams is zero percent.

The words seemed to leap off the page. Rachel felt a gasp escape her as she fell back against the wall.

"What? What?" Twyla said, her eyes wide with anticipation.

Lester was shaking.

"Thank you, Jesus," was all Rachel could mutter.

"It's not my child?" Lester said, jumping up.

"No, no," Rachel cried. She dropped the paper and buried her head in her hands as she sobbed.

Twyla immediately came to her side. "Hey, come on. This is what you wanted, right?"

Rachel sniffed and nodded. "It is. I'm just so . . . so thankful. I couldn't have done it. I couldn't have stayed," she said, staring at Lester.

Lester walked over to his wife. Tears were brimming in his eyes as well. "I'm so sorry," he muttered again.

Rachel wanted to be angry. She wanted to lash out at him for putting her in this position. She wanted to be mad at Mary for trying to play games with their lives. But at this moment she was so eternally grateful that all she could do was fall into her husband's arms.

An hour later, the tears had dried and Twyla had gone on her way. Rachel had fed Brooklyn, checked on Nia and Jordan, and now she and Lester were seated at the kitchen table.

"I can't believe Mary caused this much havoc in our lives," Lester said, still trying to process the chain of events. "And I'm not even the child's father?"

Rachel could believe it. Mary was as low as they came. "I

told you she was a conniving little witch. She probably saw you as her ticket to the good life."

Lester didn't respond as Rachel continued. "We need to call Glenn right now." She grabbed the cordless phone to contact their attorney. Rachel punched in his cell phone number and was thankful when he answered. She recapped the results of the test.

Glenn's response burst her bubble. "I understand what the DNA test says, but it's still going to be a long battle because Lester signed the Acknowledgment of Paternity. And the sixty-day period to contest the signature has passed."

Just that fast, any joy Rachel had was gone. That was why they hadn't heard from Mary in the months after the baby's birth.

"So this nightmare isn't over, Glenn?" Rachel asked.

"I'm sorry, Rachel, but in Texas any man that acknowledges paternity is responsible for the child until the court says otherwise."

"Well then, the court needs to say otherwise," Rachel demanded.

"I understand, but it's not that simple. We'll have to file a motion, get her into court and hope that we find a sympathetic judge. We have to go through the process. Plus, there's still the assault charge. We really shouldn't do anything until that is resolved."

"Oh, this is freaking ridiculous," Rachel said. They'd proven this woman to be a fraud all the way around. She'd tried to destroy their lives and now Rachel was supposed to just sit back and let the courts possibly rule against them? "I don't think so," Rachel mumbled.

"I don't think so what?" Glenn said.

She caught herself, not realizing she'd spoken out loud. "Nothing, nothing."

"The battle's not over, Rachel. But we will win the war," Glenn said confidently.

"Okay, fine. Thanks, Glenn."

She stood up and stomped out of the kitchen, not bothering to fill Lester in.

Enough was enough. Rachel had let God try to work this out, and now she was going to give God some help. She was going to confront Mary head-on with her lies.

"Rachel, where are you going?" Lester asked, following her out. "What did Glenn say?"

"He said we're still screwed because you screwed up!" Rachel slipped her shoes on. "But I've had enough. I'm going over there."

"And do what?" Lester said, panicked.

"What I should've done a long time ago." Rachel grabbed her purse and her keys.

"Are you going to beat her up?" Lester asked. "Because I don't want you getting into trouble."

Rachel huffed in exasperation. "Lester, I'm not in sixth grade. Although I should, I'm not going to beat her up. I'm going to talk to her woman to woman. And if she doesn't see I mean business, I'll show her." *I will only beat her ass if I have to,* Rachel thought.

"Rachel, I don't know—"

She held up her hand to cut him off. "You've done enough, Lester. I got this from now on."

She picked up the test results, slipped them back into the envelope and stomped out the door.

Chapter 39

Mary had just laid her baby down in his crib when she heard pounding on the front door.

"What the . . ." She looked out the window to see Craig. He had a harried look on his face and his eyes were wild. He saw her peeking out and yelled, "Mary, open up. Hurry!"

"Craig, I'm not fooling with you!" she shouted through the door. "Get out of here!"

"Open up!" he screamed, kicking the door so hard it made her jump.

Something was truly wrong. He looked scared for his life. Mary unfastened the dead bolt and cracked the door open. He pushed his way in so hard that it made her stumble.

"Close the door! And lock it!" He frantically paced back and forth in her living room. "Oh snap! Uggh!"

Mary closed the door and fastened the dead bolt. "Craig, what's going on?"

"Where's that package I told you to hold for me?"

Mary groaned at the mention of the package. She'd hidden it underneath her kitchen sink.

"Please tell me you threw it away," he said frantically.

"What? You threatened me for even thinking about throwing it away."

He slapped his forehead and started cursing.

"Craig, what is going on?" she repeated.

"Look," he said, grabbing her tightly, "you don't know nothing."

"Craig, you're hurting me! What is going on?"

Before he could answer, someone began banging on the door. "Police, open up!"

Mary's eyes widened in horror. "Craig, what have you done?"

"Just keep your mouth shut," he said as the police kicked the door open.

Before he could say a word, several officers manhandled Craig, wrestling him to the floor.

Mary watched in horror as they began reading Craig his Miranda rights.

"Miss, do you know this man?" one of the officers asked.

She didn't know whether to lie or what. "Ummm, he's an old friend. Wh-what's going on?" Before the officer could answer, Mary realized Rachel was standing in her doorway. This was the last person she wanted to see. Why in the world had she shown up on Mary's doorstep? And now, of all times? Mary didn't get a chance to confront her. An officer said sternly, "Ma'am, we're going to have to ask you some questions."

"Wh-what kind of questions?" Mary stuttered. "I'm not involved in anything he's doing. H-he just showed up here."

The officer looked sympathetic. "I understand that. But our suspect told our undercover officer he was coming here to pick up a package, so we're going to have to ask you some questions. What's your name?"

Mary looked back at Rachel, who was standing there like she was watching a good movie.

"It-it's Mary Richardson." She'd contemplated giving them a fake name, but with Rachel standing there gawking, that was out of the question.

"Okay, hold on a sec." The officer pulled out his walkie-talkie and stepped outside on the balcony as the other two officers searched Craig's pockets.

Mary felt a sick feeling in her gut as she watched the officer. His eyes widened as he looked back at Mary. She nervously bounced her leg.

"What the hell are you looking at?" she asked, after she noticed Rachel still standing there. "And why are you at my house?"

Before Rachel could answer, the officer stepped back inside. "Do you have some ID, ma'am?" he asked.

"No, I don't. What's this all about?"

The officer exchanged glances with his colleague before softly nodding.

"Ms. Richardson, do you know anyone by the name of Tammy Westerland?"

A look of sheer horror blanketed her face before she quickly recovered and said, "N-no, I don't."

The officer let out a small chuckle, then pulled his handcuffs off the clip on his waist. "Mary Richardson, you are under arrest. You have the right to remain silent," the officer began as he reached for her hands to handcuff her.

"What? What are you talking about?" Mary exclaimed, pulling away. "This is some type of mistake. I didn't do anything."

"I'm sorry," the officer said, motioning to his partner for backup, "I meant to say, Miss Tammy Westerland, you have the right to remain silent. Anything you say . . ."

Rachel looked on in shock as Mary struggled with the officer.

"No, you have the wrong person," Mary cried.

"I don't think so," the officer said. "Tammy Westerland, aka Mary Richardson, aka Lola Franklin," he added. "We ran your photo through our database and it turns out we hit pay dirt. Two crooks with one stone."

Mary was horrified as she racked her brain trying to figure out how they'd gotten her picture, let alone figured out her aliases.

"What's going on?" Rachel finally asked.

"Your friend here is being arrested for insurance and credit card fraud, and oh yeah, accessory to murder," the officer said as he snapped the handcuffs on.

"I didn't murder anyone!" Mary shouted. "Craig shot that guard and I didn't have anything to do with it!"

"You betta shut up!" Craig screamed as the police dragged him out of the apartment. "Keep your trap shut or I swear to God, I'll hunt you down!"

All of the commotion awakened the baby and he started hollering.

"My baby, my baby is in the room!" Mary cried as they started leading her toward the door.

"We'll call Child Protective Services," one of the officers said.

"No, no! Don't put my baby in the system!" she shouted hysterically.

"Well, you might want to call some relatives, because somehow I doubt you'll be coming home to play mommy anytime soon." The officer laughed as he pushed her toward the door.

Mary turned to Rachel. Her face was streaked with desperation. "Oh, my God, I know you hate me and I deserve it, but please take my baby. Please don't let them put my baby in the system."

Rachel looked dumbfounded at the request. Mary still had no idea why Rachel had shown up on her doorstep.

"Ma'am, you need to make a decision. Do we need to call CPS, or are you going to take the kid?" the officer asked Rachel.

"Take the kid?" Rachel asked no one in particular.

"Please?" Mary dropped to her knees in front of Rachel. She couldn't believe she was doing this. But when it came to her child, she had no pride whatsoever. If she had to kiss Rachel's feet to get her to take her baby, she'd do it. "You say you're a godly woman. Prove it," Mary said. She was beyond desperate. She knew the foster system all too well. She'd seen little boys in the foster system raped and turned into cold-blooded criminals. That would not be her child's destiny. "Get past your hate of me and take my child. Please?"

"Come on, lady, let's go." The officer pulled Mary to her feet, then tugged her toward the door again.

Another officer appeared in the living room. The baby was cradled in his arms.

"What's it gonna be?" the officer asked again. Rachel looked back and forth between the baby and Mary.

"It . . . it's not my husband's." Rachel meekly held up an envelope. "We have DNA results."

Mary stopped and stared at the envelope as the news registered. *Lester was not the father?* Her gut had long ago told her that he wasn't, but she didn't want to believe it. She'd even convinced herself that the doctor's timing was off. She wanted this baby to be Lester's so bad. She *needed* it to be Lester's.

"I'm sorry. I really thought it was," Mary tearfully said.

"Look, can we do this episode of *Maury* another time?" the officer said, yanking Mary's arm.

"Please take him. He's a good baby. He won't be any trouble," Mary begged. Tears were streaming down her face.

"I don't have time for this," the officer said. "Sampson, stay here until CPS arrives. We're gonna take this one on down, too."

Say Amen, Again

"Noooo!" Mary cried. She turned to Rachel again, and her voice was weak. "Please? I'm begging you, please?"

Rachel finally gave in to Mary's pleading. "Okay," she found herself saying.

"Oh, thank God." Mary's eyes flashed her gratitude as the police led her out. "I'm so sorry for everything I ever did. Please don't mistreat my baby," she called out.

Rachel automatically cradled the baby that the officer handed to her. Now what was she supposed to do?

Chapter 40

Jonathan brushed a piece of lint off his suit, took a deep breath, and walked into the church. It had taken everything in his power to summon up the courage to come. He'd been beating himself up over his failure with Roderick. He'd had to take a couple of days off from work to process how the situation could have gone so horribly wrong.

"Here you go," the usher standing at the door said, handing Jonathan a program. Roderick's smiling face filled up the center.

The family was already seated. Mr. Hurst and Rodney sat with their broad shoulders slumped. A woman dressed in all black sat between them, rocking back and forth as she mumbled incoherently. That had to have been Roderick's mother. Jonathan wondered if her intuition had told her anything about her son's unhappiness. Jonathan's own mother had known something had been eating at him, and she had even tried to get him to open up a couple of times, to no avail.

Jonathan didn't know how he endured the entire service. It had to have been one of the saddest funerals he'd ever attended. Rodney seemed to be taking the loss the hardest. It broke Jonathan's heart to hear the way he sobbed and kept saying he was sorry for not protecting his brother.

The family led the crowd out of the church after the service. Jonathan followed them to the cemetery where they laid Roderick to rest. As soon as the graveside service was over, Jonathan tried to slip away, but Rodney spotted him.

"Mr. Jackson," Rodney said, running over. His eyes were still bloodshot, and he looked utterly worn out. "I need to know, did Roderick ever say anything to you? It just doesn't make sense to me. Why would he do this?"

Jonathan couldn't help it. He took Rodney into his arms and let him release his pain.

"Rodney," Mr. Hurst said, approaching them with his wife by his side. "Get over here, boy."

Jonathan could only shake his head. Even in this man's time of grief, he was being a jerk.

"No, Dad, I need to know," Rodney said, pulling himself out of Jonathan's embrace. "I need to understand why." He turned back to Jonathan. "Mr. Jackson, was my brother gay? Is that why he did this?"

"Of course not!" Mr. Hurst snapped. "Stop saying such nonsense."

Jonathan wished that he could give them the answers they wanted. But instead he said, "Honestly, I don't know. I don't think your brother even knew. I just know he was battling some inner demons. He was so unhappy. He hated that everyone else thought he was gay. He hated the teasing. I just think he felt like . . ." Jonathan's eyes met Mr. Hurst's and he couldn't finish his sentence.

"You just think what?" Rodney said.

Jonathan swallowed. "I think he felt he was a disappointment to his parents and to you," he told Rodney.

"But I loved him. He was my twin brother," Rodney said, swallowing the lump in his throat. "I loved him just the way he was."

"I know, but the problem was, Roderick didn't love himself."

"What could I have done differently?" Rodney said, wiping his eyes with the back of his sleeve.

Jonathan didn't tell Rodney that he'd been asking himself that same question for the past week. "I don't think you could've done anything differently. I just think that he was so unhappy that all the bullying and the teasing made his life unbearable."

"Maybe I should've hit them more often," Rodney said. His brow furrowed like he was contemplating who he was going after next.

"Rodney, you fought as hard as you could. You almost got kicked out of school from fighting so hard. That wasn't the answer. Roderick just had issues he couldn't work through."

"You trying to say my son was gay?" Mr. Hurst bellowed. "Is that what you're saying?"

Jonathan couldn't believe that after everything that had happened, that was the only issue Mr. Hurst could focus on.

"I don't know whether he was gay," Jonathan repeated wearily. "All I know is he wasn't who you wanted him to be, and that caused him turmoil you can't imagine."

"So, you're trying to say this is my fault?" Mr. Hurst said, his voice losing its edge.

Jonathan looked at the man sympathetically. "Absolutely not, Mr. Hurst. All of us can stand here and ask what we could have done differently. I've done it. Maybe I should've counseled him despite . . ." He let his words trail off before continuing. "Maybe I should've seen some signs. Maybe I should've made him talk to me. We could say maybe's all day long. But the reality is that Roderick reached a breaking point."

Mrs. Hurst finally stepped forward. Her hands were clutched in front of her, wringing a worn Kleenex. "Did my son know that we loved him? Just please tell me that he knew that."

"He knew that, Mrs. Hurst. And I don't think he planned to do it. I think he made an impulsive decision brought on by the stress. Please understand, this is not a clinical diagnosis. This is just my opinion. I think he brought that gun to school to fight back, and turning it on himself was an impulse."

"Do you have any idea where he got a gun?" she asked.

Jonathan shook his head. They'd questioned everyone, and the only clue was a student who'd reported seeing Roderick talking to a neighborhood thug a few days earlier. "I'm sorry, I wish I could give you some answers."

Mrs. Hurst dabbed at her eyes. "I know people have been giving you a hard time. But keep doing what you're doing." She glared at her husband. "Keep helping children who aren't living up to what people think they should be."

Jonathan weighed her words. How could he help others when he was confused himself? Especially now that he'd been unable to help Roderick. But her words touched his core. He'd managed to establish a relationship with his own son by keeping his personal issues separate. Why couldn't he do the same with his job?

Mrs. Hurst patted his cheek. "I know you had stopped counseling Roderick. But I also know why." She glared at her husband again. "But please go back to doing what you were doing. I know Roderick isn't the only lost soul out there, and many of them have no place to turn."

Jonathan nodded. Her words gave him strength. "I will, Mrs. Hurst. I promise I will."

She smiled sadly, took Rodney's hand, then walked away. Mr. Hurst kept his head lowered as, for once, he followed in the rear.

Chapter 41

Rachel stood over the playpen and watched the little boy sleep. His thumb had made its way into his mouth and he was sucking it like it was coated with chocolate topping.

"So what are you gonna do?" Twyla asked as she came up behind her.

Rachel had been relieved when she'd gotten home and Lester hadn't been there. She'd called Twyla on the way and told her to meet at the house asap. Twyla had been stunned to see Rachel with Mary's baby.

"Did you kidnap him?" Twyla had asked.

"Of course not," Rachel had replied as she'd beckoned her in. Rachel had then recounted the whole sordid story. Or at least the parts she knew. She'd been unable to get much more information from the police before they'd ushered Mary and that man out.

"So, I'm confused. She wants you to keep her child?" Twyla said.

"A child that is *not* Lester's," Rachel threw in.

"That's some soap opera stuff, for real." Twyla hesitated. She glanced over at the playpen. "So, who's coming to pick the baby up?"

"There is no one. That's why he's here."

Twyla bucked her eyes in disbelief. "What do you mean? Don't tell me you're thinking of keeping this baby?"

"Of course not," Rachel exclaimed. "I don't want any ties to that psychopath." She began pacing the room. "But what am I supposed to do? Do I let the baby go to foster care?"

"You're better than me. I would've never taken that kid. After all that woman has done to you, uh-uh."

"You can say what you want, Twyla, but you would've done the exact same thing, especially in the middle of all that chaos. This baby is innocent," Rachel said, stopping at the playpen and caressing the bottom of the baby's feet.

"Well, even still . . ."

"I just don't know what to do. Or how I'm going to explain this to Lester."

They heard the key turn in the front door. "Well, you're about to get your chance." Twyla cracked a smile. "I would leave, but since I know all your business anyway and I'm dying to know how you're going to handle this, I'm just gonna have a seat over here." She sat down in the high-back chair in the corner.

"Hi, Rachel." Lester walked in, dropped his keys on the table, kissed her on the cheek and headed to the playpen. "That meeting with Glenn was brutal."

"How is Daddy's little girl?" he said, picking the baby up. The huge grin dropped off his face. He turned in shock. "Ummm, Rachel, what is going on? Is this who I think it is?"

She nodded but didn't say anything. "Okay, what is going on? Where's Brooklyn?" Lester started to panic.

"Calm down." Rachel took the baby from him, then laid him back down in the playpen. "All the kids are with my dad and Brenda. I didn't go pick them up."

"Is that who I think it is?" he repeated.

"It is." She pulled the covers up under the baby's chin. Then she turned to face Lester and said, "I think we should go in the kitchen so we don't wake the baby."

As Rachel headed out, Twyla followed them. Rachel shot her a look asking if she really was going to stay. Twyla shot her one right back, letting her know she definitely was.

"Why do you have Mary's son?" Lester asked when they took seats around the kitchen table.

"It is a very long story."

"I have all the time in the world."

Rachel put the tea on and began explaining what had happened. By the time she was done, Lester's mouth was wide open.

"So you actually took the baby?"

"What was I supposed to do? She was begging and screaming."

"I think it's quite admirable," Twyla threw in.

"Don't even go there," Rachel said. "Because as soon as we can get this mess straightened out, this kid is going back. Thank God the test proved he's not your child," she told Lester. "There is no reason whatsoever for that woman to be in our life."

He was looking doubtful. "So where will he go, foster care?"

Rachel shrugged. She wasn't trying to be callous. The thought of that sweet little boy being in foster care tore at her insides, but really, what was she supposed to do? "Well, all I know is he can't stay here. Maybe Mary has some family members." She gave Lester a pointed look.

"I don't know." He shrugged.

"You know, you think you'd find that kind of stuff out before you went sleeping with folks," Rachel couldn't help but add.

The look on Twyla's face told her she was out of line. Rachel had promised herself that if she was going to make this marriage work and move past his infidelity, she couldn't continue throwing the negative stuff up in his face.

"I'm sorry," she hastily added. "That wasn't necessary."

Lester nodded to show it was fine. "So, what do we do?"

"Tonight, we get some rest. Tomorrow we head to Child Protective Services," Rachel said. "I called them today. They're trying to locate a relative. I have an appointment to turn the baby over at ten thirty in the morning."

"Okay," Lester said. "Whatever you decide, I'll support."

The expression on his face, though, said he was unsure of that decision. Shoot, she was unsure, too. But she knew one thing. As precious as that baby was, she couldn't have ties to Mary Richardson, or whatever her name was.

Chapter 42

"Hey, Dad. How are you feeling?" Jonathan had come rushing over to his father's house after Brenda had called and told him that his father had had a rough night.

Simon was leaning back in his recliner, his afghan tucked all the way up to his chin. "Oh, I'm fine, son. Brenda is just over-reacting as usual. This new medication the doctors have me on made me a little nauseous."

"Are you sure, Dad? I mean, isn't there something I can do?" Jonathan assessed his father. Despite what he said, he looked sickly. His skin seemed to have lost its color and his face looked drained.

"No, there is nothing you can do. I want y'all to quit fussing over me like I'm some invalid," Simon huffed. "All I need is somebody to take me to church."

"You know the doctor said until the chemo runs its course, you don't need to be around a lot of people. Haven't you been watching the DVDs and the church shows on TV?"

"Watching on TV ain't the same as being there!" Simon snapped. He rubbed his head. "Those doctors don't know what they're talking about. I need to get out of this house, that's what's making me crazy."

Jonathan was a little shocked. His father usually didn't act cantankerous. The cancer was really taking its toll.

"Okay, calm down," Jonathan said. "What if I promise you that if you relax, take your medication—we'll call the doctor and get you a new dosage—and if you don't give Brenda a hard time, I'll come get you next Sunday for church?"

"All right, fine," Simon conceded.

Jonathan sighed in relief. He was glad his father hadn't fought him more.

"I don't know why Brenda called you," Simon said. "I know you have enough on your mind." A lot calmer, he asked, "How was the funeral?"

"As funerals go, I suppose. Roderick's twin brother is really having a hard time with it. I hope that family gets some counseling. They need it."

Simon agreed with that idea. "Yeah, that's the problem with a lot of folks. They don't want to get counseling for their problems. In my experience, God is the ultimate counselor, but sometimes you need some intervention from people here on Earth."

"I couldn't agree more," Jonathan replied. He was about to

go on when his aunt Minnie appeared. Rachel had filled Jonathan in on her run-in with Aunt Minnie, and he was praying she didn't come start in on him.

"*Intervention.* That's what we tried to do with you," she said, gazing at Jonathan.

"Not now, Minnie. Please not now," Simon said.

"So when?" she asked, walking into the room. She stopped in front of him, her hands planted firmly on her hips. "You tell me when's a good time to save his soul? You ran me off when I was talking to your daughter, and I still haven't forgiven you for that."

Simon groaned in frustration. "Minnie—"

She held her hand up. "No, Simon. I'm gonna say my peace. He's family and I should be able to say what's on my mind. You're so blinded by the fact that he's your son that you're just gonna let this sin go unchallenged."

"Minnie!"

"No, Dad," Jonathan interrupted, feeling tired. He was tired of people judging him. He was tired of beating himself up. And he was sick and tired of his aunt. "Do you think God loves me?" he asked Minnie.

"Well, um, God loves all of His children," she said. "But He doesn't love what you do," she added.

"Aunt Minnie, if you must know, I haven't had sex with a man in three years."

She gasped and clutched her chest as her eyes widened in horror. "Disgraceful!" she hissed.

"No, you wanted to deal with it, let's deal with it," Jonathan said, feeling empowered by her reaction. He stood up in her face. "You want to talk about my soul, let's keep it real. The issue isn't about me finding love. You couldn't care less about that. It's about you having a problem with the fact that I would prefer having a man pleasure me."

Minnie gasped again as she fell back against the wall and began mumbling prayers. "Just blasphemous," she muttered.

Even Simon looked horrified. But at this point Jonathan didn't care. He had to say what was on his mind.

"It's not about sex! It's an emotional connection for me. Everybody thinks being gay is about sex. It's not!"

"Okay, son," Simon said. "That's more than enough information."

Jonathan threw up his hands and lapsed back into silence.

Minnie seized the opportunity. "You didn't pray hard enough," she hissed. "You only went to the group one time."

Jonathan fought back his anger. He didn't know why he was wasting his breath, but he said, "Whether you want to believe it or not, I pray every single day. Because I don't want to be so unhappy. I don't want to end up like my student, who was so tormented that he would take his own life. A tormented sixteen-year-old. Is he in hell because he would rather die than be judged by people like you?"

"The way you are is just wrong," Minnie spat. "You can sugarcoat it any way you want, but it's wrong!"

"All I'm saying is that people should be allowed to be happy. That's what I believe God wants. And maybe you can pray the gay away, maybe you can't. All I know is so far, it's not working for me."

"Pray. Harder," she said.

Her insistence was really annoying him. "Maybe I don't need to be praying the gay away. Maybe I need to pray for peace. To be happy with the me that God created."

"God didn't create this," she said firmly.

"Why don't you let Him be my judge and jury? Maybe I will wake up one day and be cured. I doubt it, but I don't know. All I know is right now, I am who I am. But I will keep praying if that makes you happy. In fact, I'll make sure I pray for you, too."

"*For me?* You don't need to pray for me." She looked at him like that was the craziest thing she'd ever heard.

"Your sins are no less than mine."

"You can't compare my sins to your sin," she snapped. "You want to debate me on the Bible? Who you are is an abomination!"

"Okay, Aunt Minnie," he said, giving up. "If I'm an abomination, then let Him be the one to tell me that on Judgment Day."

"I'm just worried about your soul," Minnie said.

Simon finally stood up for his son. "Worry about your own soul, Minnie," he snapped. "You're so Heavenly that you're no Earthly good."

"Fine then, if you want to spend eternity in hell, then so be it," she told Jonathan.

Jonathan felt like he was trapped in an argument he couldn't ever get out of. "Aunt Minnie, I pray for forgiveness of my sins just like you do. And it is my hope that God will see fit to forgive me all of them. But until that day, I don't need your forgiveness. I don't need anything from you. If you want to pray for my soul, then I can't stop you. In fact, I appreciate your prayers. But I'll let God take care of me. I will concentrate on my own happiness and providing a good life for my son."

"Umph, you gon' raise him to be funny, too?"

Jonathan had to work hard to hold back his retort. "I'm not going to be disrespectful and say what I really want to say," he replied tensely. "But until you can learn to treat me like the man that I am—"

She snickered. "*The man?*"

"Yes, *the man*," he reiterated. "Until you can treat me with dignity and respect, then I would ask you not to say anything else to me."

"He's right. Leave him alone," Simon agreed.

"You must want to go to hell right along with him," Minnie said.

Simon fired right back, "No, Minnie, I know exactly where I'm going when I leave this earth. And I also know where you're going." He looked at his watch. "In about thirty minutes."

"Where am I going?" she said.

Simon shrugged. "Don't know. I don't care where you go, but you got to get the hell out of here."

"What?" she said. "Simon! I'm your sister."

"And that's my son," Simon said, pointing to Jonathan.

"And faults or no faults, I'm not going to allow you to beat him up. I appreciate you helping out around here, but I think we're good. So you need to pack your bags. My son is going to take me to get a cup of coffee"—he looked at Jonathan—"at a plain ol' coffee shop. Not them fancy loco mocha frappuccino places." He turned back to Minnie. "And when we come back, we sure would appreciate it if you were gone." He leaned in and kissed her on the cheek. "Thanks for everything. All right?"

"But—"

"But nothing," Simon said, slipping his shoes on. "Don't call us, we'll call you."

Jonathan couldn't help smiling as he walked past his aunt. "You have a nice life," he said as he followed his father out the door.

Chapter 43

Rachel had risen early to be at the Child Protective Services office thirty minutes ahead of her appointment time. Lester had wanted to come with her, but Sister Hicks had fallen and broken her hip and was asking for him at the hospital. Honestly, Rachel thought that was better, anyway. She didn't need Lester looking at her all pitiful. He hadn't come right out and said it, and Rachel didn't doubt he loved Brooklyn, but she could tell the idea of having another little boy in the house was appealing to him. All she knew was this baby had to go back.

She moved the car seat up front, unsnapped the baby and sat in the driver's seat with him. Last night, Brooklyn had awakened and they hadn't been able to calm her down. Not until Rachel had put both Brooklyn and Lester in the crib together had Brooklyn settled down and slept peacefully.

"You understand, don't you, pretty little boy?" Rachel said in baby talk as she tickled the bottom of his chin. "Your mama is cuckoo, and I can't keep dealing with her, because I would really hate to kill the bit—witch."

The baby smiled, and she couldn't help but smile back.

Rachel's intimate moment was interrupted by her ringing cell phone. She set the baby back in his car seat and picked up the phone. Even though she didn't recognize the number, she pressed the Talk button.

"Hello," Rachel said.

Silence, then, "Ummm, Rachel?"

Rachel grew still when she recognized the voice.

"Please don't hang up."

Rachel inhaled deeply. "What do you want, Mary or Layla or Diana, or whatever your real name is?"

"Thank you so much for taking my baby," Mary said, ignoring her sarcasm.

"Trust me, I didn't do it for you."

"It doesn't matter why you took the baby. I'm just grateful that you did." Mary sounded defeated. It was a side of her that Rachel had never seen.

"Look, I know you can't stand me—" Mary began.

"That's the understatement of the year," Rachel interrupted.

Mary continued, "But I am begging you, please don't take it out on my son. He's the sweetest little boy you'll ever meet. He doesn't deserve to be hurt because of his mama."

"What kind of evil woman do you think I am?" Rachel

asked. "You must have me mistaken for you. This baby can't help that he has a home-wrecking whore for a mother."

Mary took a deep breath. "Okay, I'll stand for that. I'll stand for whatever you want to call me. Just please don't let them put my baby in a foster home."

"How are you calling me anyway?" Rachel didn't want to talk to this woman, and the sooner she got off, the better.

"I called a friend collect and she put me through. It looks like I'm gonna be here a long time. The judge is denying bail because I jumped bail before."

A bail jumper, a home wrecker, and a criminal? Who was this woman Lester had brought into their lives?

"All I know is that I won't be going anywhere anytime soon. And all I can think about is my son."

"*Your* son," Rachel reiterated. "Not Lester's. Maybe the baby can go with his *real* father."

Mary started softly crying. "I swear, I thought the baby was Lester's."

"That's why you didn't want a DNA test?" Rachel asked, even though she already knew the answer.

"I was scared it might not be his." Mary sighed heavily. "His real father is Craig, the guy who was arrested at my house. He's gonna be behind bars longer than I will, and I don't have anyone. I don't know anyone. All I know is that my baby can't go in a foster system. Both me and Craig were raised in the system." She hesitated. "And well, you see how we turned out."

Rachel felt momentarily sympathetic, then she remembered

all the pain this woman had caused her. She remembered the taunting, the fights, how this woman had made the last two years a living hell.

"You know what, Mary? Karma is real. All the dirt you've done is coming back to you, and as the young people say, payback is a mutha." Rachel slammed her cell phone shut before Mary could utter another word.

The baby had been staring at her the whole time. He looked so innocent. He *was* innocent. *Stop it,* Rachel told herself. *Do not get attached to this kid.*

"Come on, let's go," she said, grabbing his bag and her purse before picking up his car seat and heading inside.

Rachel checked in with the receptionist, then sat in the lobby and waited for the social worker she was supposed to be meeting with. The entire time little Lester sat cooing and sucking his fingers. It's as if he knew what was about to happen and he wanted to be on his best behavior.

Rachel looked up as a woman approached her. "Hello, Mrs. Adams. I'm Aja James, the social worker who will be handling your case." She extended her hand.

"It's not my case," Rachel clarified as she shook her hand.

"Okay, handling the baby's case," Aja corrected.

"Tell me you were able to find a relative."

"We were." Aja motioned toward her office. "Come on in."

Rachel picked up the baby and her purse and followed Aja into the small office.

"Mary only has one relative, her mother, who actually lives here in Houston, and she's agreed to take the baby."

278

Rachel felt a quick pang in her heart, which she didn't understand, because this was exactly what she wanted. "Wow, that went a lot faster than I anticipated."

"I know, stories like this don't usually work out so easily. But I'm so glad it did." She rubbed the baby's foot. "God was watching out for this little one. I can't tell you how it hurts my heart to have to send a child into the foster care system. So often they never make it out and it truly messes their lives up."

Aja reached out her hand. "I'll take his bag. His grandmother should be here any moment."

No sooner had she spoken the words than the door to her office swung open.

"Hey, where's my grandbaby?" a stringy-haired, pale-skinned woman announced. She didn't look like anyone's grandmother. Deep bags ringed her eyes and her face looked hollow. She wore a dingy beige T-shirt and some raggedy sweatpants.

"Can I help you with something?" Aja asked.

"They said I could find you"—the older woman leaned back and looked at the office door—"in room 232. You the lady that's got my grandbaby? I'm Margaret."

The case worker became much more pleasant. "Hello, Ms. Margaret," Aja said. "I can't tell you how happy I am to have found a relative to place—"

"Gimme that baby," Margaret announced.

Rachel couldn't help it. She instinctively pulled the baby out of reach. Yes, he might've been her blood, but Rachel didn't have a good feeling about this woman at all.

"I'm sorry. Did you not hear her say that baby belongs to me?" Margaret asked.

Aja interceded. "Ms. Westerland, I just want to make sure that you have everything in order to take the baby home. Do you have a car seat?"

She looked confused. "A car seat? He doesn't already have a car seat? 'Cause I don't have money for no car seat."

"She can take my car seat," Rachel said, holding out the car seat with the baby in it.

Margaret grabbed the baby from her. "All right, I have to go. I don't have time to sit around here and chitchat."

The whole way she handled the baby showed there was no love between grandmother and grandchild.

"Wait," Aja said as Margaret began marching toward the door. "We need you to fill out some paperwork."

"This is my grandbaby. I don't need to fill out nothing."

"Ms. Westerland, the state really needs that information."

"For what? You got my address to send me my check."

"I really need this paperwork," Aja insisted.

"Fine," Margaret said, heading toward the door. "Mail me the papers. I got places to go, people to see."

"Can't you do anything?" Rachel asked, feeling serious misgivings as she watched Margaret walk out.

"She is a relative," Aja said, doubt registering on her face as well.

"She doesn't seem very stable. Are you sure about her?"

"She's the child's grandmother," Aja repeated.

"Did you all ask Mary, the child's mother, if it was okay?" Rachel asked.

"No," Aja hesitantly said. "Our division is understaffed and our objective is to find the nearest living relative to—"

"Oh, good grief," Rachel said, cutting her off. She stormed out of the office. She looked up and down both ends of the hallway and didn't see the woman. Rachel ducked into the bathroom, the only other place she could have gone so quickly.

Her heart dropped when she walked into the bathroom and saw little Lester, in his car seat, perched precariously on the countertop.

"Oh, my God," Rachel said, racing over to the baby. "Have you lost your mind?"

"What? You talking to me?" Margaret shouted from behind a stall door.

"You just left the baby here like that?"

"Where else was I supposed to leave it? I had to pee!"

The toilet flushed and Margaret came out of the stall, pulling her sweatpants up.

"Do you even want this child?" Rachel asked, pulling the car seat tightly toward her.

"Naw, I don't want any babies," Margaret admitted. "I don't have time for no kid."

"Then why are you taking him?"

"'Cause I need a check and my friend told me the government would give me some money for this kid." Her eyes grew wide. "Unless, of course, you want to buy her?"

"*Him,* it's a him!" Rachel snatched the baby bag off the counter, then marched back to Aja's office.

"Hey, where are you going with my grandbaby?" Margaret yelled after her.

"Mrs. James," Rachel said, bogarting her way back in the office.

"Mrs. Adams, what's going on?" Aja said, standing to her feet.

"That crazy lady left the baby sitting on the bathroom counter!"

"I had to pee!" Margaret said, appearing behind Rachel.

"And then," Rachel continued, "she admitted that the only reason she's taking the baby is so that she can get a check from the government. She even offered to sell the baby to me!"

"She's lying," Margaret said, her eyes evasive. "Now give me my grandbaby, I got to go."

Rachel looked at Aja, pleading. "Do something!"

"You know what?" Aja said. "I think I'm going to have to step in here. We have to do a site evaluation of the home and check some pertinent facts before we release this baby into your custody."

"What?" Margaret proclaimed. She started cursing and yelling, and she didn't stop until Aja called security to have her removed. The whole ordeal was mind-numbing. By the time security dragged Margaret out of the room, Rachel was trembling and exhausted.

"So what now?" she asked once Margaret was gone.

Aja sighed heavily. "Now he goes into the foster care system."

Rachel took a deep breath. She made an offer she never thought she'd make. "No, he was left in my care," she said in a hushed voice, "so now he comes home with me."

Chapter 44

"I can't keep this child." Rachel had muttered that same statement more times than she could count over the last week. She had been torn over her decision to bring little Lester home, although big Lester had been thrilled beyond belief. She had to decide this week whether she planned to keep the baby or turn him over to CPS.

Rachel had talked to everyone close to her about what she should do—from Twyla to a few of her friends on the First Ladies Council to David and Jonathan. No one had been much help—telling her this was a decision she would have to make on her own since she would have to live with the child. She'd even gone to visit the foster home where the baby would be placed. She'd watched eighteen kids there, including two sour-faced ten-year-old boys who'd tortured the younger kids while the exhausted foster mom had ignored them entirely. Rachel had left there knowing there was no way she could place the baby in an environment like that. But she wasn't ready to commit to keeping him herself either. That's why she was now at her father's house, seeking his advice.

"You know nothing that baby has been through is his fault," Simon said. He was rocking the baby back and forth, while Brenda rocked Brooklyn.

"I know, but how can I care for a child when I hate his mother?" Rachel asked.

Simon shook his head. "Hate is such a wasted energy." He looked his daughter in the eye. "I know this is a lot to ask, but have you ever thought about forgiving Mary?"

Rachel blinked and looked at her father like he'd lost his mind. "You're kidding me, right? Forgive that home-wrecking tramp?"

"Well, I seem to recall someone else being a bit of a home wrecker back in the day," Simon said with a sly smile.

Rachel couldn't believe her father would go there—even if it was the truth.

"My point is, you've changed," he continued. "You're not the same person now that you were then. Maybe Mary is capable of change. What she's gone through this last week is enough to make anyone rethink the path they're on. And the power of forgiveness can work wonders. Truth be told, it seems to me she wasn't successful at wrecking your home."

Rachel rolled her eyes. "Not for lack of trying."

Brenda finally spoke up. "Rachel, your father's right. Maybe forgiving Mary might make it easier for you to keep the child."

"Who says I want to keep this baby? I do have my own newborn, you know." Rachel pointed toward Brooklyn.

"I know," Brenda replied, "and she's as precious as she wanna be."

"Oh, hush," Simon said, fingering the little boy's face. "This child wouldn't be here if you didn't care for him."

"Maybe it's just human nature for me not to want him to go into the system," Rachel said.

"Maybe." Simon shrugged. "And maybe Brooklyn would like having a little playmate. I'm just saying, your dilemma can be solved by forgiving Mary. 'It is easy enough to be friendly to one's friends. But to befriend the one who regards himself as your enemy is the quintessence of true religion. The other is mere business.' That quote comes from Gandhi," Simon said.

Rachel waved him off. "Well, Gandhi better go on somewhere with that because forgiving that woman is not an option."

"Aren't you the one always saying you're trying to be a better person? You can do that by learning to love your enemies." Simon shook his finger at her, and Rachel could tell he was going into his preacher mode. "That's one of the greatest challenges a person can face. The hatred we feel for other people, hatred that wells up inside of us and causes destructive actions, can be overcome with forgiveness. We all, at some point or another, have people in our lives who cause us anger, or hatred or at least resentment, for something they've done in the past. But that hatred and resentment that lives within us is destructive and counterproductive."

Rachel pondered her father's words. As much as she challenged him, he always had been a wise man. But could she really forgive Mary? Somehow, she didn't think so.

"Love your enemies and pray for those who persecute you . . ." Simon paused pensively. "Have you prayed for her?"

"Excuse me?" Rachel said. She might've prayed that the hussy die a slow and painful death, but she dang sure had never prayed *for* her.

"I didn't stutter. Have you prayed for that girl?"

"Ummm, that would be no," Rachel said. "I guess you can say I'm still struggling in my walk with God, because I'm so not at a point to be praying for someone like Mary," she added when her father shot her a chastising look.

"She has some serious demons she's dealing with," Simon said.

"And that would be my problem because . . . ?"

"Because she's asking you to raise her child." Simon settled the baby on his lap, reached down the side of his chair, grabbed a newspaper and held it up. "According to this article, that girl is going to be away for a very long time."

Rachel had read the article. Mary's real name was Tammy Westerland. She had a lengthy criminal record and was now facing an accessory to murder charge, plus counts of credit card and insurance fraud. She had not a prayer of worming her way out of jail time. Plus, this was Mary's third strike, and with Texas's "three strikes and you're out" program, Mary would not see the light of day for many years.

Mary had called again yesterday, pleading with Rachel

to keep little Lester away from her mother, whom she'd just learned was trying to take custody of the baby. Mary had shared how she'd ended up in the system because her mother had tried to prostitute her when she was just seven years old. When Rachel had said that she had no desire to be connected to her in any possible way, Mary had even agreed to sign away her parental rights, since she was facing a minimum of twenty-five years in prison.

"Okay, Daddy," Rachel finally conceded. "I hear you on the forgiving, but even if I could, how in the world am I supposed to forget everything that this woman did?"

"Baby girl, it's impossible to truly forget sins that have been committed against us. Nobody expects you to selectively delete events from your memory. But the Bible states that God does not 'remember' our wickedness. God knows that we have sinned and fallen short of His glory. But since He's forgiven us, He treats us as if the sin had not occurred. He doesn't hold our sins against us. So, in that sense we must 'forgive and forget.' If we forgive someone, we must act as if that sin had never occurred. We remember the sin, but we live as if we did not remember it. Ephesians 4:32 tells us, 'Be kind and compassionate to one another, forgiving each other, just as in Christ God forgave you.'"

Rachel released a playful groan. "Okay, didn't know I was coming to church today." She guessed even though he was no longer pastor of a church, the preacher in him would never leave.

"It's always church in the Jackson house." Simon laughed.

"Ain't that right, little man?" Simon held the baby up and gently shook him. "Ain't nothing like a little ol' time religion." Little Lester giggled, then spit up all over Simon. "Uggh. Here, take your son," Simon said, quickly standing and handing the baby over to Rachel. "That's all the paw-paw time I need for today," he said, wiping the spit-up off his shirt. "That's why I don't do babies," he grumbled. "I'm going to clean up."

Rachel laughed as she grabbed the baby wipes and started cleaning up the baby. *Her son.* Could she really do it? Could she forgive *and* forget? Rachel wiped the baby down, and as he smiled at her, a voice in her head said simply, *Yes, you can.*

"But only if Mary signs those papers," Rachel muttered.

"What are you talking about?" Brenda asked. "What papers?"

"Nothing," Rachel said, smiling. "Nothing at all." She couldn't wait to get home and tell Lester that she'd finally reached a decision about what they should do. He'd be happy to know they were about to be parents again.

Epilogue

Rachel Jackson Adams believed she'd become a poster child for the slogan "You've come a long way, baby."

Rachel thought back to all she'd been through in her youth, and in the last few years. If anyone had told her this time last year that she'd be sitting in church, holding not only her child but a child that once belonged to her husband's mistress, she would have laughed out loud.

Yes, she'd definitely come a long way.

A year had passed since Mary had been arrested. She'd gotten twenty-five years. She might be eligible for parole in fifteen, but even so, she was going to be in prison a long time. Mary had signed the papers relinquishing her parental rights. She'd asked if Rachel would send her photos and maybe, if she was ever paroled, she could come visit. Rachel hadn't agreed to either. She hadn't been able to bring herself to give Mary that satisfaction at the time. But she'd realized that meant she was still harboring some hate. So she'd been sending Mary photos once a month. After all, she knew the love a mother had for her child and knew no matter what, Mary loved her son.

They hadn't had any more problems out of Mary's mother. Once Aja had informed her that the government wouldn't be giving her any money, she'd lost interest in her "grandbaby."

Nia and Jordan adored their new little brother, and he could have been mistaken for Brooklyn's twin, for the way they took to each other. Most people would think that having two babies would be difficult, but they had a calming effect on one another. They would scream and holler, and all Rachel had to do was lay them side by side in their crib and both of them would calm down.

Rachel had to be honest. She was still a work in progress when it came to the whole forgiveness thing. She'd forgiven Mary, which was the only way she'd been able to make peace with taking her child. But she still couldn't forget, and she knew that was part of the act of forgiveness. She'd have to keep praying on that.

They had wrapped up Sunday service and Rachel, Twyla and the kids had made their way into the foyer, where they caught up with Sister Hicks. "Well, hello," Rachel said, reaching out to hug the old woman. "It's so good to see you back on your feet."

"Chile, an old woman like me needs my hips. I can't even do the Stanky Leg anymore," she cackled.

"Okay, someone has been hanging around their grandchildren," Twyla said, leaning in to hug her as well.

Sister Hicks laughed again. "What gave it away?"

"Do you need anything?" Rachel asked her.

"Naw, baby. I'm just so happy to be back and to see you hung in there." She smiled warmly. "God worked it all out, just like I said He would."

"You were right," Rachel conceded.

"And you ended up with two babies out of the deal." She leaned over and tickled Brooklyn, who was sitting on Twyla's hip. "And you even got them dressed alike," Sister Hicks said, marveling at their matching purple outfits.

"No, Lewis, don't do that," Rachel said, pulling the baby's hand away as he tried to yank her earring.

"*Lewis?* Who is Lewis?" Sister Hicks asked.

Rachel smiled as she moved him from one hip to the other. "That's his name."

"You changed the child's name?"

"Yes. You know, I might've changed, but there's always gon' be some of the old Rachel brewing inside me. And the old Rachel just had to change this baby's name."

"Umph, umph, umph," Sister Hicks said.

Rachel shrugged. "You know God ain't through with me yet."

"Well, you shoulda changed that other baby's name, too. Got her going around with a name like Golden Gate."

Twyla frowned. "What are you talking about, Sister Hicks? Her name is Brooklyn."

"Brooklyn, Golden Gate, I knew it was one of them bridges."

They laughed as Lester walked over and kissed his wife's cheek. "Can you ladies hold your gossip session another time?" he asked. "I'd like to take my lovely family to dinner."

"Who's gossiping?" Twyla said innocently.

Lester shot her a knowing look as Deacon Baker came running into the foyer. "Pastor, come quick! Jordan just punched Sister Lettie's grandson in the nose."

Lester took off into the sanctuary. Rachel sighed as she shook her head.

"Aren't you going?" Twyla asked.

"Uh-uh. Let Lester handle it. I've got my hands full with these two," she said—just as Nia, who was spinning around in circles next to them, bumped into a table and sent the vase of flowers crashing to the floor. "These three," she corrected before turning toward her daughter. "Nia, get over here now."

Nia came slinking back over to them. "Sorry," she mumbled.

"Yep, we've got our hands full now," Rachel said.

Twyla laughed. "Somebody betta say amen."

Sister Hicks tsked as she wobbled off. "And with this family's luck, you might want to say amen, again."

GALLERY READERS GROUP GUIDE

say amen, again

ReShonda Tate Billingsley

INTRODUCTION

Rachel Adams is trying to find a way to forgive her husband, Pastor Lester Adams, for having an affair. Her task is made all the more difficult by the reappearance of his former mistress, Mary Richardson, in their family's church. Now pregnant, Mary claims that Lester is the child's father and is intent on seducing him away from Rachel. Meanwhile, a tragedy rocks the foundation of the Adams family and everyone involved is confronted with an ultimate decision of forgiveness.

Questions and Topics for Discussion

1. What does Rachel's dream in the novel's opening chapter reveal about her fears? How is she able to overcome these fears by the end of the book?

2. Despite Lester's continual refusal of her affections, Mary protests that the love she feels for him is real. Do you think this is true?

3. Rachel fears that her anger is interfering with her growth as a Christian. Do you agree with her decision to leave the church until Mary is removed? Likewise, do you think Mary *should* be removed from the church—or do you agree with Deacon Jacobs's assessment that "if they kicked one transgressor out, they had to kick them all out" (p. 14)?

4. Mary's visit from her mother, Margaret, is unwelcome and reinforces why Mary removed Margaret from her life in the first place. How does Mary feel when she sees her mother? How do you think Mary's relationship with her mother has influenced her as a person?

5. Mary's dealing ex-boyfriend, Craig, is another unwelcome visitor who brings "nothing but trouble" when he comes around. Is there anything Mary could have done to rid Craig from her life and leave her past behind? Or do you think her past was always destined to follow her?

6. Fed up with Aunt Minnie's constant judgment of his family, Simon reveals a few of her deepest secrets to prove that she's not as perfect as she pretends to be. As Simon says, do you think she "had that coming"?

7. Although Bobby never makes an appearance in this novel, Rachel can't help but think about him from time to time. She wonders if chasing after him in the past influenced Lester's affair with Mary. Do you feel that Rachel is right to take on part of the blame for Lester's affair?

8. After Rachel's interaction with Pastor Terrance Ellis at Lily Grove Church, she felt humiliated for having misunderstood the pastor's intentions. Did you also think Pastor Ellis was coming on to Rachel? How did you react to her reasoning that having an affair of her own would help her recover from Lester's affair? Have you ever felt a similar urge to seek some kind of revenge?

9. Did Roderick's suicide take you by surprise? Teenage bullying due to sexual orientation is a prominent topic in the

media today. How does Roderick's story echo other tragedies you've read or heard about?

10. Rachel's father offers words of advice after Lester is arrested: "Baby girl, God is in the blessing business. He's not in the punishing business. . . . Just know that God doesn't give us more than we can bear" (p. 197). Do you agree? Has there ever been a time in your life that you felt you were being tested beyond what you could bear?

11. What did you think of Rachel's decision to keep Mary's son, despite him being a constant reminder of Lester's indiscretion? Would you have made the same decision? Similarly, how would Rachel's decision have been different if it had turned out that Lester *was,* in fact, the boy's father?

12. How did your opinion of Mary change as you read the book? By the end of the novel, did you find yourself sympathizing with her situation? Or did you think she got what she deserved?

13. How does the role of forgiveness impact both the characters and the events in the novel? Is Rachel truly able to forgive Lester for his indiscretion by the end of the book? Do you think Jonathan will ever be able to forgive himself for what happened to Roderick?

ENHANCE YOUR BOOK CLUB

1. *Let the Church Say Amen,* the first in ReShonda Tate Bil-lingsley's Say Amen series, is currently being produced as a feature film. If you were in charge of casting, who would you cast as Rachel? Lester? Mary?

2. Roderick's suicide, like many other teenage suicides com-mitted by those who do not feel accepted by their fami-lies and/or communities, came as a saddening shock to those who loved him. If you'd like to help troubled teens in your area, consider taking part in one of the following campaigns:

   - The **It Gets Better Project,** a worldwide movement of hope for LGBT youth: www.itgetsbetter.org

   - **To Write Love on Her Arms,** a movement dedicated to helping those who struggle with depression, addiction, self-injury, and suicide: www.twloha.com

   - **The Trevor Project,** a campaign for a future where all

youth have the same opportunities, regardless of sexual orientation or gender identity: www.thetrevorproject .org

3. *Say Amen, Again* is the third book in ReShonda Tate Billingsley's series about Rachel and her family. If your book group hasn't yet read the first two books in the series, consider *Let the Church Say Amen* or *Everybody Say Amen* for your next discussion.

4. You can learn more about ReShonda Tate Billingsley and her books on her official website (www.reshondatate billingsley.com). You can also follow her on Twitter (twitter.com/ReShondaT).

A Conversation with
ReShonda Tate Billingsley

Say Amen, Again is the third book in the Say Amen series. Which character do you think has grown the most since *Let the Church Say Amen,* the first in the series?

It would definitely have to be Rachel. I mean, did you ever imagine the Rachel we first met would be capable of adopting the child of her husband's mistress?

Do you have any plans to write another book about Rachel and her family? What's next for the Jacksons and the Adamses?

Rachel is one of those characters that won't let me tuck her away. I never planned to write the first sequel, and she demanded that her story continue. Next up, she'll meet up with Jasmine Larson Bush, the main character from author Victoria Christopher Murray's Jasmine series. The two women are so much alike and so different and they'll clash as both try to get their husbands elected to a prestigious position in a national organization. That book is called *Saints and Sinners* and comes out in 2012.

Before you began writing *Say Amen, Again,* did you know how it would end? Was Rachel always going to accept Mary's baby into her life?

Oh, I never know how my books are going to end. That's why it's so hard for me to write an outline. My characters take over and they tell me the direction in which they want to go. So, I had no idea if the baby was going to even be Lester's, let alone Rachel's plan for the child.

Roderick's suicide is undoubtedly one of the novel's saddest moments. Why did you feel this was important to include?

I just wanted to show the tragic side of what can happen when our young people feel like they can't talk to anyone. I don't even know whether Roderick was gay, but the simple fact that he was conflicted was cause for concern. Yet, for various reasons, he had nowhere to turn.

When it comes to writing, what would you say is your greatest challenge?

Whew, I guess it would be I can't write fast enough, and I write pretty fast! There are so many unchartered territories I'd like to venture into, but my plate is pretty full. Some people would think that time might be a challenge, but I believe that you find time for your passion and writing is my passion, so time has never been an issue for me.

In its starred review of *Let the Church Say Amen, Library Journal* raves about your ability to infuse your text with "just the right dose of humor to balance the novel's serious events." Do you find it difficult to strike this balance in your writing?

I don't. At all. People are always telling me how funny I am and I just don't see it. I guess it's because I'm not trying to be. It's just a part of me; so naturally it's reflected in my writing.

When you write, do you craft your novels with a mostly Christian audience in mind? Or do you aim to reach a wider readership?

Well, I'm a Christian who writes fiction, but that's about the scope of my target. I mean, of course I want Christians to enjoy my book, but I also want nonbelievers, people of other religions, anyone and everyone to be able to pick up my book and enjoy it. And more than anything, get a message out of the book. In fact, my greatest joy in writing comes from those who found themselves growing closer to God, stronger in their faith, because of something I wrote. But at the end of the day, my message is for the masses. I believe that's what God has called me to do.

What most inspires you to write?

A pure, simple passion for telling stories.

If one of your readers wanted to write a novel of his or her own, what would be the first piece of advice you would offer?

Don't just talk about writing, write. And every minute you spend talking about what you don't have time to do could be spent doing it. So many people don't get their book finished because they let that get in the way. Something will always get in the way. The road to success is paved with tempting parking spaces. Don't take a detour in trying to reach your dream. And finally, set small, attainable goals. I started with three pages a day, five days a week. No matter what, I committed to that. Well, before I knew it, three turned to thirty and I was able to finish my book.

What would you say is the most important thing for your readers to take away from *Say Amen, Again*?

The power of forgiveness and moving past your anger. I also hope that the book helps people reflect on how judging someone is something that should be left up to God.